A SIMPLE FACT

CATHY COCKRELL

Hanging Loose Press

Published by Hanging Loose Press
231 Wyckoff Street
Brooklyn, New York 11217

Art and design by Robin Tewes. Her painting, *Hurricane,* is in the
collection of Vicki Polon and Donald Lipski.

The author wishes to thank the many individuals who have gen-
erously given their feedback on stories in this collection, espe-
cially Ellen Garvey, Tereze Gluck, Kathleen Hill, Sybil Kollar,
Robin Messing, Willa Schneberg, and Ellen Shapiro.

Some of this material first appeared in *Croton Review* and *Hanging
Loose.*

The publisher gratefully acknowledges grants from the Literature
Programs of the National Endowment for the Arts and the New
York State Council on the Arts in support of the publication of this
book. Our thanks to Larry Zirlin for production consultation.

Library of Congress Cataloging in Publication Data

Cockrell, Cathy
    A Simple Fact
    Stories
    I. Title
PS3553. O29S5   1987   813'.54   87-8677
ISBN 0-914610-45-7 paper
ISBN 0-914610-48-1 casebound

Produced at The Print Center., Inc., 225 Varick St.,
New York, NY 10014, a non-profit facility for literary
and arts-related publications. (212) 206-8465

Contents

To my sister Patty

Hold Still Now, Stacy

Dad drove. Mom talked. "Fabulous heat, pristine air, superb fishing," she said — to explain what's good about the lake, why we go there every summer. We'd gone over the pass and were down to the flat part: pine trees, orchards, farms. It was hot and stuffy in the back.

"How much longer?" I said. "I'm tired of the back."

"There she goes again," she said, like she was talking just to dad. "I called you 'Captain' in the crib," she told me. "You popped out of me headfirst and giving orders." Mom says I have a streak in me as mean as Grandpa Fitzgerald.

Amanda started whining.

"Have a pop," mom said, reaching back across the seat to neaten the bow on the ends of my braids. I opened the cooler and dug the 7-Up cans from the ice-cold water at the bottom, where the block had melted. I snapped the tops off. My fingers were icicles. "Help out, please," mom said to dad. He looked at her, just looked. He was in a good mood, I could tell. He loves projects and there was putting together his fishing poles and setting up an awning by the cabin, for shade, to look forward to.

"Hey, you twerps," he said, to get our attention. Amanda's a twerp—she was only four—but I was already ten, and going into fifth. "How many billboards are there, girls?" he asked. Sometimes we look for trees or license plates with certain letters in them.

"Not that game," I said. "I'm sick of that."

"What's that smell?" he asked, and tipped his head back to look at us in the rear view mirror. He took a long, deep brath of the smell coming in the windows. "Hops!" he said, like the science man on tv.

We left the hops fields and went up some hills. From the top we saw down the valley on the other side: miles and miles of apple orchards, and The Town. The road to Blue Hollow Lake goes through the town where my mother grew up, where her father before her grew up, where he built a house and worked and is buried next to his apple orchards. She calls it just "The Town." Its name is Colberton.

Dad shifted gears and started down, slowly, into a corridor with fruit trees, billboards, motels, gardens, houses on either side. And fruit stands that line the sides of the road leading into Colberton, made just of boards and paint and fruit crates. One time I'd seen teenagers hanging around the stands, in cars, in the dark — like they owned the stands and the town and maybe the boys had mowed my grandpa's lawn and knew things about him and called him names. Now we slowed to a stop for the light. We were at The Town's main intersection, by the gas station where we sometimes get a fill-up.

"Can we stop?" I asked. "I have to go.'

"You'll just have to hold it," mom told me. "Amanda doesn't have to go, and she drank more pop than you."

Up a side street I could see the red brick grade school my mom went to and behind it, on the hillside, the small graveyard where my grandpa's buried. He died the year I was four in the hottest week of August — "to spite the living," mom claims. I remember that from where I stood at the grave, between my parents, I saw the sopping wet circles under their arms. When I dropped to a squat on the grass my eyes came even with mom's hem, dad's pant cuffs, the vinyl bag by mom's legs stuffed with the baby bottles she still fed me from away from home. I started to whimper and saw her dive for a bottle, then the loaded nipple coming at me.

"Here, Stacy, here," she said to me, like I could suck the hurt out. She pried my lips apart, forcing a rubber nipple the color of tea between them so I had to tear it loose or suck. I pushed the bottle away, hard. She was shocked and fought back. The nipple circled near my mouth, moved in and probed at my lips again.

"Goddamn it, Stacy," she whispered against my ear. "Goddamn you, don't you make a scene."

I ended up taking the bottle, but only for a moment; when she stood up I let it drop. Afterwards, as we headed for the car, she carried me, her fingers cupping the tops of my arms and working them like a cat weaned too soon.

Mom says that graveyard's full of bad memories, like the school is and The Town, so we can't go looking around. I usually ask if we can stop. Now, just as the light changed, I heard myself adding something more: ''Can we go to the house?''

''What house?'' mom said.

''You know, *your* house! Where you lived when you were little. Where grandpa lives.''

''He doesn't live there anymore, Stacy. Your grandfather is dead.''

''But can't we see anyway? We just want to see it. Don't we, Amanda?'' I asked. Amanda nodded yes with fingers in her mouth.

Mom thought, sighed. ''If that will satisfy you, then, alright. We'll drive past. But we *aren't* going to stop. I hope that's understood.'' We turned down a side street called Poplar and drove a couple of blocks. A man was standing on the porch of the white house she pointed out. ''Look at that!'' she said. ''The lawn sure has gone to pot. And the porch. The place is a mess.''

''You can say one thing for the son of a bitch,'' dad said. ''He sure kept things up.''

''Eric!'' she said. I couldn't tell if it was dad mentioning grandpa or his saying ''son of a bitch'' in front of us that bugged her.

''Slow down, dad,'' I told him. ''I want a better look.'' Once, after grandpa's burial, mom had led me inside by the hand and planted me firmly in a tall upholstered parlor chair with wings. She sank into the matching chair that faced, just opposite. Her shoes made little black triangles like irons on the carpet in front of her. I saw her scared look and her lipstick, melted past her lips, and felt her staring at me. There was a high ceiling, a rug, stairs going up to the second floor, a kitchen at the back. I was the only other thing that moved.

Now I took the braid I was sucking out of my mouth. ''Stop the car, dad,'' I said. ''Let's ask the man if he'll let us go in. I want to see.''

''You see what I mean?'' mom said. ''Give her an inch!'' Dad

11

shook his head—at both of us, I thought. We drove past. "I'm sorry I gave in to you," she told me. "For you kids it might be just a curiosity, but for me it has a lot of bad associations. We're not stopping in The Town anymore," she said. "It won't happen." And we left for the lake.

We'd been at Blue Hollow almost a week. There were kids to play with who I knew from other years. We swam and went out in the rowboats wearing puffy orange life preservers and one day we all played on the lawn that sloped to the lake — a game called "Wounded Soldier"—Amanda's favorite game, my favorite too.

"Boom! Boom, Boom!" I yelled from the shaded spot up under the awning dad had rigged up. "Boom! Kaboom! Boom!" That was it. The battle was over, and kids all over the lawn were grabbing their arms and legs, writhing and smeared with grass stains, moaning and begging for help.

Mom came out. She carried the plastic First Aid case, with the big red cross on it, under her arm. She started with Amanda, then Melinda, then the twins, then Joel, making the rounds. "My," she said, and "Oh my, this one's bad," and "Oh dear, dear!" She was serious about her job. She bent and looked, using a piece of rope as a stethoscope to check for failing heartbeats. She made splints and bandages, out of sticks and cloth. She put medicine and stitches on the cuts.

Finally she came to me. "That's a terrible gash," she said, checking my thigh, not waiting for me to tell her where I hurt. "A deep one, just like your grandfather," she said. He had once been stabbed in the orchard by a man who picked apples. Grandpa had cheated him, according to mom. It left a big purple scar that after a while turned white. It was strange but not bad to have a wound like his, to picture him bleeding and maybe even crying. I closed my eyes tight, being him, and waited, filled up with the sound of sheets as mom ripped them into long strips. "Hold still now, Stacy," she told me. "This will hurt. But here I am. You will not die."

Then silence. I slivered open my eyes. Mom was right over me, like a big bird blocking out the sun. She looked serious, even a little scary: biting hard on her lips and winding and winding the strip of sheet around my thigh like I was a mummy. When she finished she put a finger to my cowlick and circled and circled the spot like I was the center of all things.

The next day I saw mom under the clothesline that was strung between the cabins. She was taking down the beach towels and the sheets. I remembered how she'd bandaged me, how she'd touched my head. I went over next to her. The clothespins made clicks as they dropped one at a time into her apron. She looked so thoughtful.

"I do miss my mother," she said, as she had many times before. Grandma Emily had died in her sleep, when I was still a baby. In the photos she's short and round and always makes me think of food—her garden and the things mom says she canned.

"We used to work together, just like this," mom said. "In the afternoons, when your granddad was out in the orchards. We sat in the kitchen with an enamel bowl between us, shelling the peas. Her fingers moved like this." She ran a finger down a clothespin. "Just like little plows, breaking off the peas one by one." I pictured my mom small and strong, like a tree. "She told me how she and my father first met, how quickly everything went wrong, what mean thing he'd said to her that morning. Sometimes she sang a sad tune as we worked. We were nervous about him coming back, how it would disturb our nice time, what a mood he'd be in."

Mom pressed down the pile of clothes already in the basket to make room. I watched the pile rise back up as she took her hand away and reached up toward the clothesline.

"There's a rip in it," I told her, pointing to the sheet.

"It's just at the edge, Stacy. This one's perfectly good." She knew I was thinking we could use it for the game. But only if they were ripped or worn thin would she say they were ready for Wounded Soldier. She still seemed far away from me.

"Why were you afraid?" I asked.

She knew what I meant and seemed prepared. "It was how it was. He was mean." I looked at my mom, looked at her face hard.

"How was he mean?" I asked. "What did he do to you?" She didn't answer. "Was he more mean than you?"

She snapped the sheet hard in the air. "Don't, Stacy, please.

Not today." Then, without asking me to take an end, she folded the sheet by herself. I watched it grow smaller and smaller till it was a fat square on top of the pile in the basket. Her lips began to move, like I was keeping her from what was important.

"Mommy," I said. She dropped a clothespin in her apron. I said it again. I stamped my foot and started crying. It was no use. She looked far away. She was talking, but to the sheets, the air, or someone who'd gone away a long, long time ago.

On the day we had to leave Blue Hollow I waved goodbye to all the kids out the car's rear window as long as I could see them, then sat down and opened both side windows. It was dry and hot already.

"Gonna be a scorcher," mom said. When we got to Colberton they decided we could get ice cream at the Dairy Queen and eat in the car while we drove. They went inside where it was air-conditioned to buy the cones. Me and Amanda were on the picnic benches by the take-out window, facing the main road through town. I saw my chance.

"You coming?" I asked. Amanda had an idea of what I meant. She looked back at me with big eyes. Such a goody-good, I thought. She'd only slow me down.

I ran through the parking lot to the edge of the highway. I had the light and ran across the road, then along the opposite side. I came to Poplar Street and turned down. I didn't know the house number but I thought I'd recognize the house. If I didn't, I might recognize *him*. Grandpa was dead, I knew, yet I pictured him alive — a thin old man digging out dandelions that had come up by his walk. When he stood up I'd recognize my mother's nose and her grey, hurt eyes. His chin would be loose underneath from age. His lips would be thin and tight. "Mister, do you know the way to the Dairy Queen?" I'd ask, just to get a closer look.

Where was the house anyway, and grandpa? Nobody was outside. Everyone was indoors drinking lemonade and trying to stay cool. I'd come three blocks down Poplar, running fast, and I was panting. My socks had fallen and were bunched around my ankles. I bent to pull them up. A car stopped at the curb beside me. The door opened and an arm yanked me toward the car. For a second I felt weightless. She heaved me onto her lap, banged the

14

door shut and grasped my thighs hard. Mom's face was up close to mine and flushed and like a rope being pulled from both ends so the knot in the middle stands out. I could see veins, like worms, in her temples.

"Damn it, she's impossible, and mean. She likes to hurt," she told dad and Amanda, the little tattler in the back. "She knows just how to get to me. Don't you?" she asked. "She's impossible. You," she said, grabbing my thighs and slapping at my cheek.

Then something happened to her: a sound came out of her throat, like a choke, a gurgle, and a moan all at once, and the tears that had pooled at the bottom of her eyes streamed down her cheeks. They reached her jawbone and dropped off, some of them, onto my arm. I scrubbed them away. Dad looked at us and didn't say anything, just took the turn fast, jamming me against her. When we came out of the turn she pushed me away with the heel of her hand. The car's roof was close above my head. The whole car was cluttered with luggage.

"Get in the back with your sister. Go on!" dad said. I climbed out of mom's lap and over the seat back. I felt shaky and strong and glad. Amanda stared at me from her corner by the cooler, like she hoped to see me cut down. "Stop staring, jealous," I wanted to crow. She was still a baby and could only watch.

We sped away from Colberton, swerving out from behind horse trailers and apple trucks to pass them. Mom's face looked slack and red, like a new apple gone soft in the sun. As we passed through the flatland, the car veered suddenly.

"Oh Christ!" dad swore, and pulled the car into line, then over to a stop.

Amanda and I stood in the dry, knee-high grass by the side of the road while they changed the tire. Behind us was a huge field of grain, its color shifting—tan to gold to tan—with movements of air. The car looked solid; I wished I were inside it; I felt light and alone, about to be blown away. Dad cranked the jack till the wheel spun free of the ground. Mom rolled away the bad tire and helped fit on the spare. The muscles in her forehead bunched together, as if in sympathy, while he tightened the bolts snug. There was sweat by dad's mouth. I felt red heat in my own cheeks—not sunburn, but panic and relief, that *this,* at least, they still could fix.

15

Travelling

It is the mother who does the travelling out through the world of city streets with its signs and turns, the cars and crossings, vendors and yelling. Carrying packages she looks a bundle herself, winters, wrapped in a long wool coat.

A father, thin and fastidious, owns a soft wine-colored ascot. He likes a few well-made things he can barely afford, folded in precise ways, kept in particular places. An ordered world he rarely leaves except to follow the same, sure route to his work. The man is never seen outside his neighborhood. "He has a phobia," the mother explains. She dies, pneumonia, and he cannot go to the hospital.

The daughter, living two years later in the care of a godmother, travels alone, weekends, across the city; the steps of the streetcar are high. The father's room, attached to the back of a big house, has its own door and lots of windows. Newspapers are piled near the foot of a simple bed, on a deep wood chest covered over with a grey quilt. The father always seems glad to see her when she comes to visit.

"Enter, little friend." There are bottles in the window—blue and green. His forehead is high, his temples hollow with a raised vein leading down his cheeks, half covered by the hair. "Hey you, Junebug." His name is Burt. Kicks back, stretches out on the bed, lanky, sets June up on the spread beside him. The kid's tentative, wondering. Full of grave doubt, she imagines him still at home if she were dying across town.

Blue bottles with the light coming through. Green. The light falls on the dark wood, the newspapers, the black lace-up boots set beside the bed. The windows are held in a hundred square frames. The purple beech outside the window shimmers in the light. When he's in a mood he plays piano on her stomach—runs and chords, a choppy boogie woogie.

Sometimes he props himself on one lean elbow and the kid.... She sees the hair fall against his brow. When he's at his ease, she combs it. Its tangles separating. Soft. So close. The comb's teeth are fingers, all her fingers, pulling through his hair.

How does he read June's silence, the hopeful hesitance on her brow? She listens, unsure, and Burt so near. A stir: beech leaves beating against themselves outside in a windy sky. Father. Burt-burtburt.

They happened one day to open the chest — the grey quilt pushed away, the cedar lid lifting up. Revealing. Not revealing. Simply there.

Junebug leaned over the side of the chest and looked. The chest gave up a smell of pitch and wood—like a forest with all its dark unnoticed crooks where branches join the trunks — the smell of those places, individual yet similar. June's hands flexed open, midair, above the open chest. There was the black photo album, so close. Boxes of buttons. A big pointed yellow button June had forgotten, but recognized, from a coat her mother once wore, singing as she fastened: "Button up your overcoat, when the wind blows free...." Would he let her touch the things that might take her — or him — to some other place? *He has a phobia.* There would be other times; there would never be another time.

Burt watched the kid, frozen over the chest, its box of buttons, its combs, the album of photographs, a hat, the brooches and slips. He felt a danger. He fished up a single, faded photo. She, eager, took it from his hand. The sky pale, the woman's skin pale, the trees, in contrast, dark and fierce.

On the back, the mother's penned script, smudged on one edge: "This is me and a poinsettia bush and a beautiful white dog at the city gardens." Her head thrown back a little. A leg pushed forward. A petalled flower, from the bush, in her hand. And the scant clothes so overexposed that the dog was partially indistinguishable against them. Hard to imagine: she looked so unencumbered there — no bundles, no signs of worry.

Burt studied the picture for instruction: should he let June take it? Alright, he seemed to decide, but nothing else. June saw that the wood lid had suddenly come closed again; the grey quilt was arranged on top. June lost the chance to touch the things, was saved from them again, except for one small, significant snapshot.

The blue bottle. The beech leaves purple-green. Shimmering. His dull-colored hair, lost eyes. His wine-colored ascot. "Au revoir, little friend."

June travelled back across town, the steps of the streetcar high. Her godmother waited in a house without spots, odors, or pets. The world was behind. Its solaces and dangers. The city gardens. The father. The unencumbered woman. The stark white dog.

The Beautiful White Dog went between the leaves of a book. Was home.

When June came back the next week he did not answer to her knock. The lock was undone and the door swung open. She stepped into the room, its smell of wood and of his particular brand of cologne.

Late afternoon, turning to evening, the room darkening and the windows so still between her and the purple-blue back yard. June thought of walnut meats, the high, then deep, places hidden back behind the membranes. Water in the bottles. Yellow-green cologne inside its container.

She inhaled, searching for changes: how long Burt had been away; the things he cooked himself to eat—fried potatoes, coffee. She couldn't smell those things, nor whiskey from the half-full bottle near the bed. But when she took the cap off and leaned over the bottle, into the smell of liquor: the bottle tipped, the whiskey flew through the bottle's throat, biting as it reached the back of her own—something she would not dare except *Burt, where are you out in the lost world you stay away from?* The liquor scalded its way down, swallow by swallow, till she perched, then sank, into the stuffed chair. She felt happy, as if listening to Burt while he lay across his bed, his head against the low, rear bedstead. Time, she imagined him saying, could run out any day!

"Look, Junebug, there are things I've never said. I don't know why, I've always meant to and wanted to give you at least that." A hum sound comes out of him, as if in answer to the reproach or hurt in her guarded eyes. *"I*

did. Look: do you know the earliest thing I know about myself? They say I was walking with my mother, no older than four.''

June remembered the high reach of her own arm to her father's. She was three. Her legs performed the miracle of walking, a bit wobbly, mother of the man, for he was wreathed in the smell and sweat of alcohol and more unsure on his feet than she, as she led him along.

". . . They cracked up. They said they'd never heard a kid say anything like it.''

She imagined Burt finishing his story of being four, and that she had missed almost all of it! Mad at herself, then him.

"Father, it's not like you ever gave me practice at such things—listening —my head so stuffed with what it makes up. . . . Burt!

But he hadn't stopped, she imagined. He was still recalling: the house he grew up in; its smells; how his sister, dead Aunt Priscilla, had looked and acted; how June's mother was.

June drew her legs up close on the cushion, nodding asleep and generating heat and pictures that came in waves, the room closed out behind her eyelids. She slept and dreamt.

Burt came home. Threw on the lights, drank from the bottom of the bottle, heaved himself onto his bed. He watched June's fitful then heavy sleep, pressing a finger against his lips.

The next time, from the top, battered step, the doorknob was reachable, but locked. *Father, let me in.* Strange for him not to answer; he did not work Sundays. "Burt, let me in, please.'' She shook the dorknob. Thought she heard him stirring inside. Or was it the branches of the beech tree? A random piece of rubbish moving in the yard outside his windows? He had his curtain drawn across the low panes, the ones she was tall enough to peer through. The glass bottles stood dull-colored against higher panes, some filled part way up with water, and cuttings of plants stuck in. "A glass of water, Burt.''

The sound of Burt's feet inside the house, against the floor boards. The wood vibrated under her feet as he approached. She felt the door's motion as it opened, making a wedge of his life visible. A slightly smaller-than-usual wedge?

"Junebug! How are you?''

She saw the bureau, the wood chest, a bit of his stuffed chair, and part of a woman's leg. And 'enter little friend'? Instead he opened the door wider, gestured her on in. She met a lady with red hair. It grew in waves, like the hot red waves of color you might see through your eyelids on the beach. Her smooth, crossed legs. Her rust-colored hem. Fingers curled around the ends of the stuffed chair's arms, as if crushing a flower. A dark fur coat lay on the chest, touching the foot of the bed near Burt. There remained the hint of some rich, burnt color it had once been. It was matted and June watched a single ravelled thread hang from its lining, against the quilt. A cloth handbag with a big flower print, its sides gathered at the top onto sticks, was at the foot of the chest.

They were only a coat, a handbag, a lady, June told herself. Because they seemed to have some weight and life of their own: not a coat but a familiar, furred animal that lay sleeping, exhausted, on Burt's wood chest; huge-headed hydrangeas and mums that massed together on the floor. It must be the lady with red hair who gave them their life. Maybe she had a whole world of such things: china cups, glass butter dishes, records she sang to, her voice clear. She was so pretty.

June felt a for-no-reason bashfulness. She saw some hint of trouble in the deepest, low places of the lady's face. Burt's spare, neat space grew cluttered with their unasked questions. Against the press of them, the woman's legs stirred; the hem's waves moved. *Thank you, lady.* Because the woman broke the silence.

"I'm Clara."

"I'm June."

"You've come a ways. Would you like a glass of water?" The water trembled in June's glass as she held it. Waves of trouble and color and the dull overcast day. June lifted the glass and drank, its thick bottom holding Burt, distorted, in her view. Burt on one elbow, watchful, but this time so intently watchful. Worry was caught in Burt's face; his limbs were twisted together in an unfamiliar, awkward way.

"Junebug," Burt said quickly, "this is my new wife." That scrabbling look of his. The clouded way that Clara looked back at him. "I've been telling her about you. Showed her the photo album." June felt pleasure, distrust, and bashfulness. She imagined Burt proud, his new wife politely looking at the photos— June at ages two and three. There was something wrong with it.

21

Would he really pull out her photos, show them off? Or had Clara found the thing and asked Burt? With her red hair singing had she wanted to know more about her stepdaughter, the one in the photo with sand on her knees?

"Who's this, Burt? Our girl?"

"That's my June, my Junebug."

Oh Daddy! Lady!

Clara watched the kid's knotted, bothered face, the thick way she had begun to breathe. Clara seemed to know about that, somehow, because the troubles in her own face appeared to move and shift.

Oh lady, mother, don't go sour! But Clara did not go sour, fade away, disappoint. Her live red hair, animal coat, the flower bag remained.

Burt said "Isn't it about time, June? Won't Grace be worrying?" Burt was not fond of Grace, June's godmother, and had never cared a whit for what worried Grace. June felt it, did it show? Because Clara said something right away.

"Shall we walk together and wait for it?" *'It,' What?* June must have asked, without asking, because Clara said "the streetcar." *Oh yes, lady.* June must have smiled, because Clara smiled. Burt did not smile. Something else moved through him. He said—no, did not say, but gestured, or started to. As if to tell Clara "don't go"? *Is that it, Burt? "Don't go." And "no." And "no."* That word he'd answer, round and full of its precise gravity, if you asked him "please" or "join me," if you looked back, or showed you needed. It would form in his face even before it fell from his lips, heavy and inevitable. The word he sometimes did not even say out loud yet seemed to say. Like this time, as if Clara would hear it and hold back.

Instead she lifted her coat from the chest and slipped into it. As Burt, abruptly decisive, got his own coat from the corner chair, got Junebug's, feeling June's delight and reproach, it seemed, because of his shabby explanation: "Got to work the Junebugs out." Lights out, the door slamming behind them as they traipsed across the flagstones with the bordering tufts of grass. The intimate sounds of the back yard behind them, saying a goodbye.

And the feel of it. Not Burt's and Clara's expressions, nor even the cut of their bodies against the air, but having Burt travel so far out in the world. *Is it because of Clara, a beauty, who you call your wife? Is it true, with mother, when she needed, that you let her die? You just standing there at home. So useless. So she died. And can't you even see it now, how Clara needs? And me, too, father, can't you even see?*

He did not say. The houses stood in a row, close together like a fist. Soon they would reach the place where the streetcar stopped, just before the corner statue of the martyred general with its streams of pigeon doo and of pale green running down the darkened bronze. Clara in her long wintry fur. Burt in his salt-and-pepper wool coat, his ascot, and his lace-up boots, looking thin and towering. June, feeling his silence, his hand stiff in hers, looked apprehensively for traces of the fear that might be overcoming him. And to think he had changed, maybe. Because of Clara, perhaps, his beautiful new wife, he called her. But then again, maybe it was only because Clara had come. And Clara, did she understand these things? Did she know others, secrets?

They had reached the stop, where the streetcar waited. June had to rush to get aboard. Out the window, as the streetcar began to move, she saw Clara and Burt turn back toward his house. And saw the martyred general's pale green tears as the car passed by him, carrying her away.

Nada

Sometimes even still I look for her, the way I've seen her mother Mannie do a thousand times, studying a stranger's face for the characteristic crease leading down from the nose and around the lips, the precise line of her profile. It happened last night while I was retaping my handlebars. I had one eye on the evening news, where they showed a Las Vegas casino under investigation, shots of men and women at the slot machines. I realized I was scanning the picture for my long-lost friend; I felt empty, then pissed off.

I turned on the radio, a "Remember the Beatles" marathon, sang the ones I knew. I stared out the window at the pink neon, across the street, advertising auto parts, wondered what to do with myself. Mannie says it's dangerous and unchallenging for me to keep being a bike messenger, can't I find another job and a nice place to live. I tell her why bother, that I stay at the Y because I'm leaving any day. She gets a scared look in her eye. She puts my name on mailing lists for the local colleges' catalogues and sends me little notes about jobs she's seen advertised. I just throw them out. She's clutchy and it makes me itch.

Another tune came on and I sang to it. The words made me feel better; they were like a sign: "I said even though you know what you know / I know that I'm ready to leave. . ." That was me talking back or at least telling myself what to do. It's time to leave you, Nada, leave the city. If I don't have Golden Gate Park to go to, then I won't have to remember the rowboat we capsized there, you mad and blaming me. I'll never go downstairs to the pool and picture you again at six learning to dog paddle, pink cap close around your eager, puppy-like face.

25

I pulled the shade down and got into bed. I fell asleep and had a lot of scary dreams that I couldn't remember this morning when I woke, except for the fact that they'd been about Nada. We lived next door to each other growing up and were like sisters; we stayed thick as mud clear up through high school, despite the three grades between us.

But when she graduated from high school she got accepted to a college in the Midwest. She hadn't even told me she'd applied to someplace far away. She promised me that we'd stay close. In the letters she wrote her freshman year she said she'd joined a group, some sort of political action committee against the war. The next fall, just before Thanksgiving, an ROTC building on her campus was bombed and Nada disappeared. She's still at large and "Wanted." All the rest, by now, have gotten off, or are behind bars, or have done their time and been released.

As for Nada? The Underground is under ground, I imagine, literally. I imagine her living in tunnels under some city, part of a small society of derelict winos and bag ladies with feet wrapped in newspaper pages cursing at old adversaries or babbling in duck sounds. I picture her watching, holding her breath against the smell of urine, babbling and ranting, too, in duck talk. Or I picture her dead.

I tell myself then, stop it, Jess. You know her better than that. You know better than to paint her into such a seedy, desperate scene. So I make her conventional: hushed voices and dry rattle of popcorn boxes. In my mind she leads me down the sloped theater floor. I pay attention to her long brown hair, so like her mother's, swaying against her back. The resemblance is there in her face, too, as she stops, turns, and directs me to a seat. Her flashlight arcs away and she goes back up, leads others down for revivals of "Woodstock" or "Fantasia" or "The Way We Were."

So Nada is an usherette at a movie theatre in Minneapolis or Dallas. She's the secretary at the B&J Realty in Portland— Oregon or Maine. She xeroxes leases and answers phones and glimpses herself in an office mirror, accustomed now to the dye job and makeup that have changed her looks. She stares at the coffee in her styrofoam cup, nibbling teeth marks into its edge, remembering, maybe, the photo that *The New York Times* refused to print — two Americans staring horrified at a Vietnamese with a napalmed face. Or the anger in the air as the action was planned — the throwing of blood, weeks before the bombing. Or the R.O.T.C. officer's expression as the blood splashed in his face. She's remembering me and wondering if I went to college; if my mother moved to the Southwest like she always said she would; if I've moved out, travelled, or married.

She's remembering her home and parents: Mannie shouting "dinner!" down the basement stairs or out the door into the foggy evening air, or Daddy coming up out of the basement rubbing off of his hands the bits of airplane glue and Spanish moss and modelling clay and tiny artificial shrubs that Nada gave him for his train room every birthday all the years she was growing up, as she could think of nothing else.

Nada had known only one story from Daddy's childhood: that his sixth grade teacher had asked the class to write papers beginning "I wish I were . . . ." "Eighteen years old," their themes answered; "teacher's pet"; "a drummer." His mother had saved his — that's how he remembered at all. On a rectangle of lined paper it said only "I wish I were not here."

Crow's-feet crimped at the corners of his eyes when we reminded him of what he'd wished for. With a toothpick from between his teeth he would pick a pun we'd all heard before: "cantaloupe" as "can't elope." Or he'd poke me in the ribs calling me "Second Daughter" and saying I should call him "Daddy" like the rest of the family. He said Mannie could be my second mother to make up for mine who was always at work or "out," as she put it, with one or another of a long string of boyfriends. He'd be my second father, he said, because mine had been killed in a car accident when I was three. Or he'd poke Nada with the crust of glue on the end of his finger saying "Nada, I'm stuck on you" with a mischievous self-congratulatory giggle. Then Mannie would shatter the brittle patter by belting out a line from "South Pacific." She did it without any sign at all except to dig deep into the well of gravy in her mashed potatoes or more determinedly into her salad.

"She's got a song in her heart and a frog in her throat," Daddy would quip then. He said it quickly to smooth over his wife's oddness and then he'd look at me to see how I was taking it, and at

Nada to judge her expression as she poked her fork tines into her pork chop, brooding—on the singing, the puns, a scolding, or on the sting of Daddy's hand the time she spilled the beans, told me that Santa who came each Christmas with carved soaps was not Santa but her Daddy, really, and if you came into the basement you could even see his suit.

"Look, the jacket with the white fluff trim! The beard with the carpet beetles in it! The black boots!" Nada was worldly then and I was shocked. Daddy spanked Nada hard and she wasn't allowed to play with me for a week.

It's not as if going underground was her first disappearance either. Once she got lost for hours at Disneyland. And disappeared again on a trip to Yellowstone I took with them the summer after her freshman year in college, not long before the bombing. Nada was nineteen and strikingly beautiful, I thought. We stayed up most of one night and she told me things about college —about Marxist professors and student activists, the strait-laced Administration, the study groups, and surprise actions protesting the war. It was hard to imagine when you were still stuck in a high school where VFW speakers at assemblies drew standing ovations. I felt jealous, also grateful that she'd told me, and excited.

But then the next day Nada refused to go look at a single geyser, walk any of the trails, or attend the ranger's slideshow talk. She did this two days running, kept disappearing into the campground to, quote, take the pulse of America, unquote.

The second night she disappeared again, left me alone in the tent with Mannie and Daddy and a camplight that glowed inside its glass flame cover from a fragile, sock-like filament. He pumped up the pressure tank and read *Newsweek* aloud and Mannie cut and did all her nails including toenails. Then she said she was going to fetch "that daughter of ours," did anyone want to come?

Silver Airstream trailers crowded the campground. Women sucked beer from brown bottles. Boys on banana seat stingray bicycles popped wheelies on the roads that wound through the campgrounds, roads we followed seemingly for miles till we found her at someone's campfire, talking about draft resistance, and we brought her back between us. Mannie seemed frightened.

She talked at Nada hard and angry. Nada fell silent. She wouldn't speak a word; she was not there — not for Mannie, not for me. And I wasn't there, as far as Mannie was concerned; she just kept speaking to Nada in a steady, nonstop lecture.

That night we lay in the dark, my sleeping bag next to Nada's under a black sky thick with stars. She slept with her arm flung out of her bag and I held it — tentative, mixed up, angry. I could hear Mannie and Daddy talking in their tent, not their words but their voices. On the sloped sides of the tent I could see tall shadows of Mannie and Daddy created by the small filament that gave off intense light and broke into ash if it was ever touched.

Mannie is waking up across town, I imagine, in the twisted sheets between her husband's side of the bed and the photo of her daughter on the nightstand. She rolls over, opens her eyes, sees the early morning sun falling on the pillowcase. She identifies the noise, his Lionel train, that is coming through the air vents from the basement like it did when we were kids and I was sleeping over. She touches the dent Daddy left in the sheets when he rose and went downstairs, sits up on the edge of the bed, shuffles her feet into her fuzzy slippers. She pads across the carpet past the bureau's clutter of perfume bottles and hard plastic combs.

In the bathroom at the sink she splashes sleep from her eyes, moves her lips in small worried speeches. She says "hello" shyly in the mirror to an imaginary new face at the Unitarian church where she goes Tuesday evenings to a film and discussion series: "The 1960s — Decade of Dissent."

"Hello," she says, and then a quaint "How do you do?" to a vaguely familiar girl who in a momentary fantasy (for she has confessed it comes in daydreams, too) is Nada Returned, though barely recognizable, thanks to the years of separation or the skill of some plastic surgeon in reshaping Nada's features — Daddy's cheeks, Mannie's nose.

Mannie assesses her face critically in the mirror. She swings the mirror open to get at the medicine cabinet behind it and remembers that when Daddy opened the door that day the news crews already had their cameras rolling and their questions ready: "How do you feel? Would you say your daughter was rebellious? Do you expect to see her again?" Mannie had come to the door to see what was going on and was standing right behind him. When he didn't answer they asked her.

She says reporters hounded them mercilessly for days, trailing mazes of cable and shoving microphones into their faces like so many flies waiting to sting. You dared not push them away, Mannie says — they would broadcast that too, or put it on the front page under sensationalistic headlines.

That first night she witnessed the wreckage on national news: firefighters tromping like moon men over the splintery rubble of blackened bricks and timbers. There were burnt blueprints and books with delicate charred spines and black ash pages. There were the broken bone shards of the security guard who had a wife and four children and was killed instantly, just like the life that was taken away from us, she says, and replaced by this cross we have to bear. Your reputation is a precious, fragile thing, she always warns, and offers herself as proof. She asks me to imagine turning on my tv and seeing a picture of myself, sobbing, and to feel like she did the judging eyes of viewers all across the country.

And Daddy's been no solace, she has confided. She says his model trains are growing into something like an obsession, as if he's getting prematurely senile, as if corpuscles in Daddy's brain are withering right up. "Oh spare me," she begs him now, when he starts the puns. I remember the look in Mannie's face across the table the time she told me that — the despair, vulnerability, and anger in her eyes, the pressure inside of my not knowing what to say.

I see Mannie locating a gold gadget and crimping her eyelashes with it in the mirror. She carefully smooths Oil of OLAY across her cheeks and chin. The eyelash curler and the open bottle of lotion remain on the counter when she leaves the room. At the kitchen sink she runs the water over last night's dishes, testing its temperature with her fingers. Her eyes are focused out the window on the fog churning in and nestling softly against the eucalyptus, the pointy-sworded yucca, the hedge, making the whole yard look blurred and muted. "Like us," Mannie tells herself, "like Nada, like all those angry young people searching for themselves who led our Nada astray. She was so suggestible, a victim of her time. But who knows? Maybe she'll turn herself in this year, and a quake will shake off all this fog."

Mannie, humming, pushes the faucet toward the row of drying cups, the upright silver forks, the spoons, the bone china plates leaning in the drainer white as skeletons, as bone fragments. "Stop it, Mannie," she tells herself out loud. She taps a plate with her fingernail to hear it ping, a sound distinct from that of bone: solid, not hollow; hard-edged, not porous; clear and distinct as you, too, may learn to be. No more like you're still stunned and bumbling around in a fog, tangle-headed as a clump of Spanish moss pretending to be trees, dead as bits of it falling with the flecks of glue off Daddy's fingers at the table, in the bathroom, even on the goddamn sheets.

"For Christ's sake," she probably tells him, "if you're going to touch me there, no scratchy flecks of glue on your fingers, alright? No stiff little reminders of your miniature world down there that you rearrange and shape. It's just the two of us now, safe between the sheets — your touch familiar, your calves hairy, our limbs so tangled up I can hardly tell arm from leg from ass from your far away elbow to your thick lost wrists to my withering brown tit." But he's somewhere else. "Then look," she'll tell him. "You cannot see? Then give me your hand. Feel my hip. Think of it, if you must, as a knoll behind the miniature depot. Feel this Spanish moss between my thighs. Just let go and lose yourself, like you do in the train room for hour upon hour, never bothering to talk to me, upstairs alone."

Mannie has told me that Daddy is this way because of the bombing, that it's all because of Nada. But she's simply forgotten. Even years ago I can remember Daddy emerging from the basement with train tracks in his eyes. Now he tells me he has a recurring dream where he is hopping freights across the country. He marvels at how effortless it is, how the flatbeds seem to spread their laps to him invitingly. No boxcar bums bother him or threaten murder. There are no inspectors, no arrests, as the train pulls away from the city and the skyline opens up and work, obligation, shame, and loss fall away.

He says the last of the tenements give way to warehouses scrawled with graffiti, as the train picks up speed and dusty bushes beside the track flail messages in the rush of air — celebration or alarm, he can't tell. Then basement refuges are no more, he says, and Mannie doesn't let loose with any spontaneous belts of song to tell him, in so many words, "You're dead and I'm alive, la, la," and there are no more memories of hippies, the war, the protests; no more Nada growing more lovely and more a stranger, sexed and dangerous, no more Nada in the headlines. All of this dissolves, Daddy says, and he feels free and punless.

I go across town to Mannie and Daddy's on a little visit, hoping that perhaps Mannie will have stepped out on an errand. The last time I saw Daddy alone I felt a small change in him. Sitting upright in bed among the rumpled sheets and cast-off newspapers he was attentive, even a bit affectionate.

He told me he'd been reading up on the anti-war movement. He was irate at the media portrayal of the '60s protestors. He had once met and compared notes with the parents of two others in the Underground, a brother and sister. He had seen their high school graduation photos too. He had stared at the newsprint reproductions of them but he couldn't for the life of him see a "dangerous revolutionary, possibly armed" or his own daughter, still with baby dimples in her cheeks, as a raving outside agitator. As he told me about it he pulled on his sideburns and I wanted to reach out and touch them. I thought they would be soft as cotton on a baby's face.

Mannie has invited me to one of her Tuesday evening programs on the 1960s. I ring the door bell and hear someone coming. The door opens and it's her. I hear the tv and see Daddy on the sofa watching. Mannie says "Come on in, how are you, Jess?" tousling my hair. "It's a special on earthquakes," she explains. A San Francisco building inspector is talking about cornices that will fall off and kill people if a big quake hits.

While Mannie gets ready I eat the meatloaf and vegetables she's reheated for me. I imagine the people who'll be there tonight as a bunch of parents and hip psychologists trying to get in with young people. Just to see this scene I've agreed to go. She tells me about the leader—such a nice young fellow. He's well informed and has chosen some excellent films. It makes you more aware. She says she's sure I'll like it. I'm sure I won't.

Mannie talks at me as she drives. She asks me questions.

About rock music, drugs, and the Marxist-Leninist parties. About anarchists, libertarians, socialists, Trotskyists, Maoists. I have heard there are differences. I tell her everything I know, I make up things I don't—eagerly, as she values my information; desolately, to think I'm her medium in a dragged out, ritual seance, a window on her Nada.

Mannie parks the car. We walk a few blocks to the church, passing a derelict rummaging through a wastecan on the sidewalk. I look at Mannie and am struck again by the family resemblance. I laugh at myself for imagining that Nada and I have never actually been parted, and that just now it's she who's walking by my side. I think what a crazy piece of world I am, and imagine astronauts looking down on Earth and a dot called ''San Francisco'' where life goes on and may one day be shaken completely apart.

Inside Mannie exchanges greetings with people who have been coming to the series. They look the way I expected—lots of beards and little mustaches on the men, brightly colored skirts and shawls from south of the border on the women. I figure most of them must go to this church and I get the feeling that Mannie has told them who she is and who her daughter is, and that it's the subject of some interest.

A woman wearing expensive silver bird earrings and an ''Arms are for Hugging'' button approaches Mannie. Others nearby keep talking but seem to listen. Did Mannie see in the paper today where another radical has turned himself in? The AP speculates that the Underground is experiencing some changes. Perhaps it will have some effect on Mannie's daughter. Maybe the discussion leader will know more about this.

It happens quickly. I watch Mannie's face, only a while ago glowing in anticipation of the evening, now anxious and conflicted. I feel a small surge of hate, and wonder if that's what I'd feel for Nada if she came walking through the door. Several people are talking to Mannie—about the woman's news, I think. I wonder whether part of Mannie isn't delighted at this development, and if she hasn't been liking all along the attention that Nada has brought her. She looks up momentarily with a distressed expression—might I get her a cup of water from the fountain? she asks — and submerges again into the conversation till we're told it's time to begin and we take seats in a room just past the hallway.

The leader explains the film we're about to see. It's about a housing struggle that took place in New York City in the late 1960s, he says, and some of the political groups they talked about last week played a part.

He turns the lights out, the projector on, and the film begins. The opening shots, from the air, show the ruins of the South Bronx — acres of roofless shells and empty lots, street grid, then the river, Manhattan beyond, more Bronx, then a dense cluster of buildings where hundreds of Hispanic tenants, the heroes of the film, conduct meetings, carry signs, hold out to win a long, grueling rent strike.

"Be here now," I keep telling myself, but I can't concentrate. I keep dozing off into dreams where I'm lost, walking down streets where shattered glass glistens like beach sand. There are fires, and people dragging pieces of furniture to shacks they're constructing between the remnants of brick buildings. The shadows of birds in flight move with a kind of magnificence across the tall exterior walls of gutted buildings.

I feel the distant motion of people leaving the room; the far-off sounds of energetic, interested voices; the high cold presence of the overhead lights.

I follow the last of the people out into the hallway. I notice illustrative posters pinned to a bulletin board—one saying at the bottom, simply, "Madame Binh" and the other "The Whole World is Watching: Chicago 1968." Looking around for Mannie, I catch sight of her leaving the church building absorbed in conversation with a woman who has recently befriended her and, I imagine, knows what she's been through.

On his way out the door a professor type winks at the leader and kids him: "Venceremos."

I step outside, and hesitate, figuring which way to go to reach the Y. One pyramid-shaped building cuts a wedge in the skyline, braced as if it means to survive a quake and stand alone, amidst the rubble. It's dark out, and I start walking.

A Simple Fact

The place they rented for the summer was the top floor of a tall, ramshackle house on Lawrence Street, by the river. From Libby's room, off the kitchen, she could survey the world: a corner of the garden, a length of the freeway leading to downtown Eugene, the back yard of the young couple who sometimes let Vy and Honey and Libby borrow their van; in the other direction, across the street, a corner of the house where Leif lived, an elderly man who fed them tea and graham crackers in his parlor. She could see both sides of the blackberry bushes that separated their place from a dirt yard and yellow house where two small black boys lived with their father and a miserable hound.

The boys had been digging a hole near the fence, and whenever they played there she could overhear them talking. The younger boy, Junior, was a giggly child quick on his feet. He was good at ducking when his older brother James tormented him by hissing "wart juice" as he brandished an open palm. James possessed a tinny but apparently indestructible transistor radio that he wouldn't let Junior touch—although once the older boy forgot it by the hole. Then Libby heard the radio go on, and Junior singing "When A Man Loves a Woman" to it from beside the sticker bush.

Now Libby saw James alone on the back porch, whittling savagely with a pocket knife at a stick, dipping and bobbing his head to the music coming from his radio. From behind the screen door, the father appeared, said something, and the boy threw down the whittled stick and reluctantly went in. She'd only seen the father outside mornings and evenings, when he left the dog in the back yard a bowl of food. The man was stocky, low to the ground, the color and build of her mother's oak dresser, and he said things to the dog that Libby couldn't catch, or maybe it was understand.

Libby laid out four kites in a row along the floor—two eagles, one hawk, and one flying dragon. She left them there to dry and went outside, found the trowel where she'd stuck it in the dirt. She started weeding around the tomato plants. The ground was moist and black and seemed fertile. It made her think about Indians gathering blackberries and hazel nuts in this same spot near the Willamette River one hundred, two hundred, maybe a thousand years ago. It was one of those ideas dad had indoctrinated young minds with at his Cascade Camp for Gifted Children—or "glodded clods," as she called them. Every summer since she was thirteen Libby had helped the child prodigies identify their dead butterflies and build reflector ovens. They'd have to label and mount her, like their ratty Lepidopteras, if she worked there again. She'd be that dead. Instead she'd moved to Eugene with her new friends from college.

Libby turned the soil over with hard twists of the trowel, thinking how sick she was of kids, and glodded clods especially, and tossed the weeds into a small pile between the plants. A high-pitched voice she recognized said "What you doin', lady?" Libby searched at ground level between the berry stalks, and when he added "Over here!" she spotted the set of eyes peering through the brambles.

"Junior!" she said, to surprise and baffle him.

"Hey, how you know my name?"

"Oh, I know. I know everything," she said automatically, before she even realized.

"You do?" His eyes went wide.

"Oh yes. I know everything about you, Junior."

"Like what?" he asked suspiciously.

"You got a brother James. You got a dog," she told him, changing the way she talked. Embarrassing, actually, if one of her roommates had heard, or the man. With Junior, who was six, seven tops, she could try it out.

"Hey, what you doin'?" a second voice said to Junior, and a second face peered at her through the vines.

"James, she knowed your name," the little boy told him, and

Libby said simultaneously: "James, why'd you quit your whittling?" Her question, she thought, sounded innocent enough.

"Gone," was all James said, clearly impressed.

"What's tomorrow?" Junior tested Libby, who had come closer to the blackberries and was looking at them through the stalks.

"Saturday," Libby said.

"No, I mean, what day is it? What special day?"

"Birthday, you mean," Libby guessed.

"Hey, you got it, lady," Junior said. "James' birthday," as James socked his brother soundly behind the vines.

"Ouch!"

"I know," she said.

"You knowed it was my birthday?"

" 'Course."

"You get me a present, lady?"

"Libby. My name's Libby," she said, thinking that he was a little wheedler, and also that those kids didn't have much, hardly even clothes, no bat or anything, much less bicycles.

"Bibby, ribby, dibby," Junior said.

"If you knowed it was my birthday then you got me a present," James persisted.

" 'Course I did." She could think of something for him. He always looked forlorn.

"Hooboy," James said, which was about the most excited she could imagine him sounding. "You bring it over?"

That could be weird. "You come over. In the morning. I'll give it to you then."

"Hey, you stinkers, get out them ladies' bush!" The boys hopped away, startled. What was with their dad? Libby wondered again.

James whispered back hopefully: "We be there."

Junior asked one final: "You know stuff?"

"I know all about you, Junior."

Libby gave James one of the kites she'd constructed out of rice paper and sticks and string. Too fragile and too subtle, she thought, as she brought it from the closet, placed it in his pink, waiting, upturned palms. He'd much rather have a bright mylar

Superman dimestore thing. But when James opened his eyes he turned the kite over and over with wonder, while his little brother hopped from one foot to the other and reached for it, envious and amazed. James pulled it back, ran his palm under his nose and wiped it on his blue jeans.

He wore tennis shoes and a short sleeved shirt with the bottom button missing, so his stomach poked through. The pale track of a former part ran in a straight line along his close-shaved head. Junior wore cutoffs. His bare arms were thin and small, the color of espresso, and Libby wanted to touch him. She took hold of his shoulder to steer him around the apartment as she answered his questions about Honey's autoharp, an African violet, her serape. With James, who had just turned ten and was big for his age, Libby felt less free. They came into the kitchen, where Vy stood at the counter studying the drink book — full of recipes for Pink Ladies and Gin Fizzes and Brandy Alexanders—they had found at Goodwill. As James spun the kite around from a short length of string in the center of the room, Vy looked up.

"Jimmy!" she said.

"James," he corrected.

"James, is that your dog?" Vy asked, pointing down through the window at the boys' yard. Libby thought she knew why Vy, who was always grumpy and silent before noon, was being so chatty. It was the same reason she always found herself talking, sometimes saying the stupidest things, when she was with black people: she wanted to show them they were wrong, that their color didn't matter to her; she thought they didn't like her and she felt afraid. Libby felt a little sorry for Vy just now, yet glad Vy asked about the dog because she couldn't ask herself, on account of the game she'd started with the boys.

James nodded solemnly, still intent on his kite.

"Is not," Junior countered. "He daddy's dog."

"What's his name?"

"Spinner," James said. But Libby wondered if Vy had meant their daddy's name. Vy was as curious now as she about the father. Leif had just told them how the man had gotten hit in the head in a logging accident, had sustained brain damage, and had never been right since. Every so often you'd see his head make funny movements; he forgot things; they lived on disability, Leif

38

said. James had let more string out and was spinning the kite around, knocking the bookshelf.

"Hey, James," Libby said, "don't knock things! You go fly it outside, OK?"

James was agreeable, even elated, as if till then he hadn't quite believed it was his. The two boys clattered down the steep stairs that clung to the side of the building. Junior tumbled the last three steps to the ground, picked himself up, brushed the dirt off his scraped elbow without a whimper. Libby sucked in her breath when a car braked swiftly for them as they darted across the street. She watched them race down the broken sidewalk till they reached the field by the river. That was probably the end of the kite.

Libby was in the front yard painting her bike with red Rust-Oleum. It didn't make sense, really. The bike was a junker she'd bought used. It would last the summer and then, when she went back to school, she was going to leave it. But this was fun, anyhow, and it made it hers. She stepped back to assess her work, using a palm to push loose strands of strawberry blonde hair behind her ears. James was calling to her again from the strip of grass by the street where he and Junior had been playing. She saw a place she'd missed on the part going back to the rear wheel. She took another dip of paint, crouched to brush it on.

"Come," Junior said, from right beside her. He was bare chested and barefoot. Beads of water sparkled in his hair as if he'd recently come from the river.

"Hey, man, what chu doin'?" she said.

"Hey, man," Junior imitated. "James say come." He grabbed her hand and yanked. She pulled back long enough to lay the brush across the top of the open paint can. Junior led her to where James was bent over in the grass, his eyes wide with fascination like some little glodded clod unearthing fossils.

"What you doin', James?"

James straightened up suddenly, a small, badly wounded pigeon struggling in his hand. Libby jumped back. Ugh! Don't show you're scared, Libby. But it was too late; James had seen it and he advanced, holding the half-dead mangy bird upside down by its tail and swinging it at her.

"Heehee," James cackled. Junior squealed, hopped down off the curb. A dark car gunning up the street crossed the intersection; another bolt of fear electrified Libby.

"Gotya!" James yelled. Junior squealed once more. The car barreled on south. The bird lay on the pavement. "Eeeee!" screamed James, staring, as the pigeon made a pathetic effort to get up on its feet.

Libby stood fixed, caught between the impulse to run back to her house and the desire to come close to study the bird as James was. He was poking at it with a short stick as if he were dad pointing out the parts for the edification of the campers.

"James!" Libby said, from back a ways. "Why'd you throw it? Do you feel better now, James?" When he didn't answer she stepped forward and pulled back his forehead till he had to rotate, look up at her from his crouch. "That was not nice!" she said even more sternly, wishing that by towering over him and by raising her voice she could make him listen. "Why'd you do that? Why'd you do that?" she heard herself ask another time. He was trying to gross her out, she told herself.

"Bird juice," James jeered, yet bent ceremoniously to circle and circle the pigeon slowly with the tip of his stick. It was down on the ground again, though not quite dead, she thought.

"Ick!" Junior squealed, but bent to look, as James did, with an almost scientific concentration. When she reached the sidewalk and looked down Lawrence Street and saw that it was empty, she was sorry. She wished a car would hurry up and run over the pigeon and put it out of its misery.

"Need you" was all Junior said the next evening around dinner time when he came for her.

"What for?" Libby said, not turning from the tomato bush she was staking. Endearing, Junior's answer, as if he'd read her mind: "Not birds!"

She found herself following Junior out of the yard and along the sidewalk toward the house next door. Another trick maybe; or the black man sick or injured or maybe drunk; James hurt by the stove or the dog.

The grass in front of the house was scruffy and strewn with pods from a bush beside the walk. Libby remembered being seven, and another walk like this one, when someone had dared her Halloween night to trick or treat at Robbie D'April's house. Every little kid in the neighborhood was afraid to go near there because Robbie had been to reform school. Libby took the dare, had gone alone down the walk while the kids stood in a clump by the street and watched. When she passed the holly bush obscuring the porch from their view, she had slipped behind it and waited, trembling.

But then she'd been a child, and now she was nearly 19, so she kept on walking all the way to the porch this time—where Junior swung open the screen door, then the inner door, and gestured at her to come in. She thought of the father and she thought of old Leif across the street, watching her probably with shock and disapproval. She tapped on the door, knowing she was about to see the man seated in his chair, wearing slippers, and wall pictures of Martin Luther King and John F. Kennedy, and that the next record to drop onto the turntable would fill the room with the sounds of James Brown.

The boy looked at her questioningly. She stepped in. There was a couch, a tv; there were windows facing the street, and discolored orange curtains pulled across the bottom half of each, making the room dim and giving it an orangey glow. The floor was linoleum, a white and green swirling pattern, and squares of it were missing. Libby noticed everything she could, would have lingered even longer, to feel what blackness was.

But there were two doorways leading into other rooms, and Junior motioned her through one of them into the kitchen. James was seated by a table that held a plate of cooked hot dogs, two place settings, a jar of pickles, a juice bottle filled with green Koolaid, and more dry Koolaid mix spilled and sparkling across its checkered surface. He had a large bottle of yellow mustard in a vise grip between his knees and was straining to get it open, his face in a knot that eased when Libby came through the doorway. James held the jar out to her. So this was it, her lowly mission. She remembered not to show surprise.

"Alright, then, here we go," she said, as if to distract them from her curiosity. The walls of the room were bare and dirty white. There was a metal cabinet over the sink. "Take a photograph, it lasts longer," kids at camp used to say, if you stared.

41

That's what she half expected James to tell her now. She felt ashamed. And she sounded to herself like she was thirteen still and hardly older than the eggheads and maybe not as smart, yet obliged to act it for weeks and weeks and weeks.

"We having a picnic," James said, and waved his hand over the meat and the fluffy white buns.

"So get them ready. I'll get this off if I can." The boys happily laid the hot dogs in their buns, then stacked them back on the plate. Libby turned on the hot water tap and let it run. Junior stood on tiptoes on a chair and pulled a third plate and a cup down from the cabinet. The water turned hot. She held the metal lid under it awhile, removed it from the water, popped off the lid and deposited the jar with aplomb on the table. Each boy slathered mustard on a hot dog. James took another, prepared it, and deposited it on the third plate. He poured her Koolaid and pointed to her chair.

Libby ate the hot dog; she even drank the Koolaid. There was mustard now in globs on the table and a thin smear on Junior's face and James' shirt. From James' radio a DJ was counting down the top 40.

"What you been up to?" she asked them.

"Nothin'," James said.

"Weren't you just down at the river?"

"Yeah, we go there."

"It's fun?"

"Fun," James repeated, and Junior said: "Real fun. James and me go dippin'."

"You like summer?"

"It's alright," said James, spinning the dial, coming back to the same song. Libby cut another hot dog in half with a serrated knife, the kind you got with cereal box labels.

"Where's the girls?" James asked.

"Oh, around," Libby said of her roommates, and asked back: "Where's your daddy?"

'He with Phyllis Dillis, at the store," Junior chirped. Libby knew from the way he put it that Phyllis was not their daddy's girlfriend, even as the picture that came to her automatically, like images on a huge wrap-around movie theater screen, was of two bodies on a couch, the woman's hand on the hairs below his navel, the blackness of their skin, the open-toed high-heels in a little heap on the floor.

"Who's Phyllis?"

"Aunt Phyllis," Junior said, and in an instant Libby revised her picture of their lives. She saw they had an extended family in town.

"She's your daddy's sister or your mama's sister?"

"No," said Junior. James said: "Daddy's."

"Oh, and where does Phyllis live?"

"On the moon!" said James and giggled—or maybe laughed at her. Junior was overcome, too; he laughed till he choked and spit out bread bits. James thumped him on the back.

"Do you visit Phyllis?"

"Yeah," said James, between bites of his second hot dog. "We going there today." Junior ate Libby's other half. She watched James dutifully push the remaining hot dogs together on the plate and place them on a shelf in the fridge, like a little man. James left the room and Libby watched Junior eat. With her own food gone, she had no excuse to be there and nothing to occupy her hands. When James came back with the kite she'd given him, in surprisingly good shape considering, she welcomed it.

"Got broke," James said. "This part here." He pointed to the cross string that the bridle attached to. Libby saw that it had come untied from the end of the stick. She re-secured it. Then she saw Junior run to the front door and down the walk, toward the car that had pulled up. Through the kitchen curtains she saw the man getting out of the car and Junior greeting his dad. Libby half wanted to slip out the kitchen door and cross the back yard, where the dog was, into her own. She saw the father rubbing Junior's head as they came up the walk. She couldn't just sit there and let things happen to her. She got up and stood in the doorway between the kitchen and the living room, holding the kite like an alibi or a shield.

Junior and his father came in. The man was compact, and thick around the middle, like she remembered him, and looked potentially powerful. He did not seem shocked.

"Hi," she said, sounding as stupid as possible, she thought.

"'lo," said the man. He threw a paper sack down on the chair by the door. "You give the boy that kite." Libby didn't understand if it was a question, an acknowledgement, or a reproach.

"Yes," she said, admitted.

"Was real nice," he said. She noticed the slur to his speech. "The boy can't fly it right." He looked at James with what she thought was affection, but James lowered his head. Now she couldn't see his eyes. Poor James! And his father didn't mean it that way. Libby wished she could stop everything and explain: 'James, what your daddy meant was. . .' "Got no one can show him," the man added—putting himself down, or her, she couldn't tell.

"Get ready," he told the boys. "Phyllis be right back to get us." It seemed the man didn't understand *her*, either, when he turned to her now saying "Gotta take the boys," as if apologizing; as if she and his sons were best buddies.

"Them kids like you. . . ." The man paused to find her name.

"Libby," she said.

"Libby," he repeated. "Junior say 'Lippy'," he laughed.

"What's your name?"

"Tyrone." He held out his hand. Libby took it. Such a black name, she thought. The man seemed very black to her; she didn't know what she meant.

Tyrone sat down in the chair by the door and pulled up a sock that had bunched down into his shoe. Libby sat on the couch opposite, still holding the kite between herself and him, herself and the room. She looked around to see it again from her new vantage point, and quickly, before it all went away. Tyrone wore light grey loafer-style shoes and dark green polyester pants, a white crew neck T-shirt under a pale green cotton shirt that hung open. Light caught the top of his hair; he had small shreds of white in it, like a kid who'd been rolling in the dust. James came in from the back room with two small baseball jackets, dropped one over Junior's head, then sat on the couch by Libby and Junior.

All four of them, now, were sitting in orange light. Tyrone's lower lip, that showed pink, was cracked and his skin was lighter just below the cheekbones, darker at the temples. Every so often his chin turned to the side, over his shoulder, then lifted, in an involuntary motion. Libby felt sorry for Tyrone, and frozen in place, trapped between going and staying.

She stood, and felt tall and exposed, though she was only medium height. She pointed a toe at a square of linoleum, then back at the one behind, then to the right square and the left as if absorbed in the rhythm. This was what had happened to her, just because an adult had arrived, even though she'd been told he was half simple. Front, back, side, side; if the boys noticed she could count on them to react somehow.

A car honked from in front of the house and Tyrone stepped out quickly. The rest of them went out, too.

"Come Lippy." Junior pleaded. "Come to Phyllis.'"

"You're welcome," said Tyrone, as they went down the walk. "Please. You can watch the kids." Maybe he didn't consider her their playmate after all, but their babysitter. Still, it didn't matter. A week ago, for the fun of it, she and Honey had snuck onto a roof at the University of Oregon with blankets. They lay out under the stars singing a round Libby made up about a gypsy girl and a magical beggar boy, till they fell asleep. Only Sunday she'd gone to a service at a nearby Pentecostal church, just to see what it was like. Libby could do what she wanted, and now she wanted to do this.

"That there," said Tyrone, and dipped his head down and pointed through the window of the beige and brown two-tone Pontiac, "'s Phyllis."

Libby ducked and smiled through the glass, pulled the back door open. The woman at the wheel forced a smile. "Come on, Tyrone," she growled. "Ain't got all day."

"Girl's coming too," Tyrone said as he opened his door.

"Now I seen everything!" said Phyllis.

"She wants to," Junior started to plead, but Phyllis interrupted.

"Suit yourself, Tyrone. It's your day." She crushed a cigarette out fiercely in the ash tray, then added: "They named you wrong, Tyrone Speed; you slow in every way. If you make Ross late, can *you* do his job? Who*ever's* coming, just get in."

Libby crawled in the back, and Junior behind her, then James.

The car's interior was dark brown and cavernous. Phyllis put the car in gear and whooshed away from the curb. Phyllis' head, poking up above the seat, seemed yards in front of Libby, like when she was a kid and they'd gone to family drive-ins in the station wagon—her mom and dad in front, she and her two sisters in the back.

From her angle Libby saw that Phyllis wore purplish lipstick and purplish rouge. She had gold hoop earrings from which dangled flat gold Ps and her hair was done in loose, oiled curls. "Hush you," Phyllis said over the seat at the kids. Libby sank back, deep into the seat, into the farthest corner of the car. It was OK. If she were in front between Phyllis and Tyrone she wouldn't know how to act. She thought she'd feel stiff, and that if she looked right or left, at either of them, she'd smile nervously. She stretched her legs out straight and undid a button at the top of her blouse, as if relaxing.

Phyllis was one of those experienced drivers who took the blocks fast and the stops hard. She could handle the car with her left hand when she needed to do other things with her right. Phyllis fished on the seat between her and Tyrone and something made a click, and music came on, a woman singing "My Funny Valentine"—the same song Libby's mother listened to on her Frank Sinatra albums. Phyllis sang along. Her voice was deeper than Libby's mother's—an alto maybe. That song ended and the singer started naming all the seasons she loved Paris in.

They pulled up on a residential street. "Now everybody stay put," Phyllis said sternly. "You kids: there's glue on them seats and you can't move." An old joke, it seemed: Junior and James started giggling uncontrollably and groaning forward and falling back in their seats like they were being sucked back by glue. "You, too, Lippy." Junior said, and she did it too.

"You want to fetch him, 'rone?" Phyllis said. "And tell Ross it's near past seven. He better move."

Tyrone took the cement steps up to the house in twos. After a minute, three at the most, he came back out of the house with the other man. Tyrone returned to his side of the car, Ross to the driver's side so that Phyllis was forced to scoot to the middle. Tyrone went to sit down.

"You sit on my tape machine, I'll kill you," Phyllis warned.

"Wait," said Ross. "This won't work. Tyrone, you get in the back with them two kids."

"Three," said Phyllis, and gestured at Libby. Ross looked

back at Libby. The muscles in his forehead and just by the bridge of his nose moved with surprise.· "Don't look at me," Phyllis said. "'Rone's idea."

Ross just quietly said "hello" and Libby wished she could explain to this man—this sensible man, she thought—that it was all their idea, not hers. They started driving through the streets again till they caught the freeway.

"So what's the story?" Ross asked Phyllis.

"I know? 'Rone's little thing," Phyllis said, as if Libby didn't have ears or weren't there.

"You're bad," Ross chuckled.

Libby wanted to ask how much further, to know exactly, now. But she figured it was like walking past a barking dog: go slowly and don't show you're afraid. If she started drawing attention to herself, they would know she was scared. They continued east toward I-5, then south on the interstate.

They pulled up in front of a store in a little town somewhere in the foothills of the Cascades. Ross looked at his watch, said it was just past nine. Libby would have guessed later; it was dark anyway. Honey and Vy would be home by now and Vy would be making them hot buttered rums. Libby wished she were having one with them. I am somewhere near the mountains in a big car with a black family—poor black family, she said to herself. A simple fact. It did not feel simple. Ross took his lunch box from the floor by Phyllis' feet and said goodbye. Libby was sorry to see him go.

Phyllis got back in the driver's seat, looked into the back. Junior and James were asleep and Tyrone didn't budge to move up front; he just kept staring out the window at where Ross had gone. Phyllis mashed her lips together tight and put it back in drive.

They kept heading east or south, it seemed. The evergreens lining the highway got taller, a deep black tunnel they were driving into. Just this regular family, Libby said to herself again, slowly, evenly, and they're black—to see if by saying it that way she could feel it. She thought of one of the old songs she had played at camp, the one the junior high kids liked: "It's a long, long road/from which there is no return/. . . He ain't heavy, he's

47

my brother.'' The song made it sound simple, like the rouge on Phyllis' cheek: you could rub off the rouge and there'd be black; then you'd rub off the black and there would be humanness, Libby thought, everyone the same.

Phyllis reached to the dash, waited for the click, then held the red coils of the lighter to the end of the cigarette between her lips. The car tires hissed along the highway. It had started to rain.

Libby sat at the table in the middle of the room, facing the low black wood stove and the black and rust-colored stovepipe that rose straight up and took two angles before it disappeared out the sloped roof. Junior started kicking her under the table. She told him to cut it out. Like the Speeds' house in Eugene, there was a doorway in the center of the back wall leading to another room. The walls were rough wood; the floor was planks. The roof was corrugated tin and the rain beating down made a commotion over their heads.

Even though it was summer it was chilly here. Phyllis put in papers and kindling and lit the stove.

''You hungry?'' she asked them all. She took a covered pot out of the fridge, put it on the stove, heated it, poured thick pea soup into bowls. While they ate she plunked down at one end of the couch, by a tv tray taken up by a framed photograph of a teenage boy, and lit a cigarette. Phyllis looked weary, like the boys were, and Libby was.

When they finished eating, Phyllis told James and Junior to wash their faces. To Tyrone she bunched up her brow in a serious, disapproving look and nodded toward the boys, at Junior on tiptoes reaching for the spout. Tyrone hurried over to the sink to help, the same way he'd hurried to the door on Lawrence Street when Phyllis first honked—like he had to prove to her over and over that everything was under control, that he could function as a father.

''Had your fill?'' Phyllis asked Libby in a gruff voice.

''Yes, thanks.'' Libby wanted to ask when she could go to sleep. ''That your son?'' she said instead, glancing at the photo. Phyllis nodded. ''How old is he?''

''Nineteen in August.''

''He lives with you?''

"Sure. Most time. He up in Portland this summer to his cousins'. Selling 'cyclopedias. Door to door."

How interesting, Libby thought. The boy was up at her home and she was down at his. He must look different this summer; in the photo he looked like someone white people would be afraid to open their doors to: tall and defiant, wearing a billed cap backwards. She looked at the photo and saw all the black kids in high school, who'd had their own particular sections of the halls, the lunchroom, the nearby streets. They and the white kids never mixed. You never knew what posters they had on their walls at home or what they talked about at dinner.

Phyllis closed her eyes—as if to end the conversation. When the kids were washed up she told them to go in to bed. "Get it toasty for Phyllis," she actually said; it was the nicest thing to come out of her mouth all day, Libby thought. Phyllis brought two wool blankets, threw one on the couch and the other on the cot she'd brought out, and went to bed. Within minutes it was silent back there; Phyllis and the kids were in dreamland. Libby heard the rain and the crackle from inside the stove. Phyllis had damped it down before she turned in but you could still hear the fire inside. It seemed important for some reason to tell which sounds were the fire and which the pellets of water crashing on the roof. Tyrone, on the cot, took slow draws off one of Phyllis' cigarettes.

Libby tucked the blanket in around her shoulders and put her face into the back crease of the couch. She envied the boys, their aunt, all peas in a pod. After she was four Libby never slept again at night between her parents and she wondered if she'd missed something; at the very least she was missing something now, she figured. It was hard to think of things switched like that. Tyrone finished the cigarette; she could hear him mash it out by the sink.

"Libby," he said, from over there. She didn't answer. Tyrone took a step back toward the cot, hesitated. "Libby, you awake?"

He came over by her, bent, and put his hand on her shoulder. She could feel it through the blanket. His hand was big and the shoulder he put it on was small, like at Delta Epsilon's final bash, where she'd gone for kicks and gotten drunk on their beer and cheap wine and ended up in a top floor room with a creepy jock and had done it with him. She could still feel his hands on her. If

49

she hadn't been drunk she would have been afraid, and now she wasn't drunk and she didn't know Tyrone either and he was black and they were somewhere in the woods in the middle of nowhere and it wasn't going to be day again for hours. She could keep pretending to be asleep or dead.

"What?"

"Libby. You're such a pretty little girl."

"Thanks."

He moved his hand to her forehead and held it there, like a parent judging a child's temperature.

"Leave me be, Tyrone. There's no room here." Tyrone didn't move. "Please," she said. Tyrone lowered himself onto the edge of the couch. She felt he wasn't going to go away. "You're just lonely," she told him. "You want somebody just to touch you? Is that all?"

Libby sat up and reached out of the blanket and laid her arm woodenly across to where he sat, dense and motionless except for a rolling twitch of his neck. She still felt sorry for him, even now and here, she thought, and resented him for making her feel that way, for being black and fucked up so that she couldn't just hate him like she could the frat guy. And even if this was all he wanted, was she going to sit in this frozen little pose till morning? Tyrone placed his far hand on her arm, just above the elbow.

"Please leave me alone," she said, one more time, starting to cry, and then decided to get up off the couch. She crossed to the cot, took the blanket off it and left the cabin, darting through the rain. She went in the front door of the car, locked it, then locked the driver's door, climbed over the seat and locked both back doors. She saw herself being quick, methodical and thorough; she felt both on her own like a pioneer, and all alone. Rain was pelting the roof. She wished she had a set of keys. She could play the radio. Or drive home. If the cops stopped her for car theft, she'd tell them what had happened; they'd send her on. She made one of the jackets the boys had left into a pillow and lay down on the seat. It couldn't be much later than midnight.

She heard him outside the car, tapping on the window, gesturing, trying to tell her something. She rolled the window down a crack.

"Sorry, Libby," he was saying. "Sorry."

"OK. It's OK. Go to bed."

"Libby, sorry." Rain streamed off his hair, his sopping shirt and down the windows. "Please. Come back in. I won't bother."

Something made her believe him. She unlocked both doors facing the house, in case, slammed the car door behind her, lifted the blanket out of the water as she went. She got back on the couch and wrapped herself in the blanket. For a little while, shortly before dawn, she slept.

Everyone got up late, and they had some left-over biscuits from the fridge. Phyllis made the bed in back while Tyrone folded up the cot and the blankets. Then they all got back in the car, in their original seats. Libby slumped in a half sleep against the left rear door she now thought of as hers. She felt brittle, achy with exhaustion and, at moments, near tears. When Phyllis turned the ignition key, the motor ground and ground, almost caught, then died, ground and ground again, and died the same way.

"Bastard," Phyllis said, and tried once more, listening hard for when it caught. But the beast wouldn't go. Phyllis got out and lit a cigarette, stood with her arms folded a few feet away.

"We glued?" Junior cried out after his aunt.

"No, stupid," James said, as he opened his door calmly and got out. "We broke down." Tyrone got out the front door, then Junior got out, snatching after his father's hand. Through the front windshield Libby watched Tyrone and Junior cross in front of the car. Tyrone fished a cigarette from Phyllis' pack on the hood, lit it and went back over and sat down on the porch step.

She couldn't believe them. Why weren't any of them even opening the hood? She started making up mantras in her head out of songs and kiddy rhymes: "One, two, buckle my shoe/three, four, shut the door. . . The bear went over the mountain/the bear went over the mountain/the bear went over the mountain/to see what he could see."

Libby rolled down the window and hung her chin on the lip of the glass, staring at Phyllis. Phyllis didn't make eye contact, just smoked. Libby got out of the car.

"What we gonna do?" she asked, trying to sound calm and casual.

"Do," Phyllis repeated in flat declarative. "What would you

51

suggest? We gonna wait or pray. She'll come 'round. Usually does."

Pray, Libby thought. What a joke! She could see it now: "Dear God, something is wrong with their car. Would you mind checking it out? Please, you understand. Thanks a lot."

The sun was cutting through the trees in strong, warm, slanting beams. Phyllis stared hard into the sunlight, over the tops of the trees, and puffed. Libby sat on a stump and stared too—her side to Phyllis, her back to Tyrone. She was ignoring Tyrone. Phyllis crushed the butt in the dirt and walked, real slow, back to the Pontiac. The engine ground again; then it caught. Libby wanted to cheer. She'd been rescued. Everybody migrated back matter of factly and got in. The car bucked down the dirt road over the pits of water left from the rainstorm.

The Pontiac was the first to arrive at the county park, then a red car followed by a teenage boy riding a motorcycle and, awhile later, a small blue station wagon. Libby was introduced all around—to Tyrone and Phyllis' handsome brother Vernon and sister-in-law Diane and their two little kids and older son. Also for the second time to Ross, who'd come straight from work in the station wagon with a man wearing an orange shirt.

They staked out two picnic tables at the top of the park, above a sloped clearing. Everybody else in the park was white: the family nearby cooking over their fire pit; the man with a big grey dog, assembling a fishing rod; across a small clearing, just past the bathrooms, the five men drinking beer in lawn chairs around a smudgy fire.

Junior darted to the edge of the site, where a pair of chipmunks were chasing each other up a tree trunk. Libby went over next to him. The chipmunks paused and she made noises to scare them into motion again. Junior was still yelling excitedly up into the tree as she went back to the others, sat down at the end of a bench. She tossed a fir cone at James' feet, then was glad she'd missed. She didn't really want to play with them anymore. She hardly wanted to talk. Still, she felt glad when Vernon took a seat across from her, twisted open an Olympia and offered it.

"So where you from?" he asked.

"Eugene. Next to Tyrone's. How 'bout you—I mean originally."

"Right up here. Born and bred." He took a drink of beer, sat silently.

"You like it here?" she asked.

"Oh yeah. It's pretty up here. Don't you think?"

"Real pretty.' They both got quiet again, Vernon thinking his thoughts, Libby trying to see it—who Vernon was, who they all were. "Ever been away?"

"Yep. In the service."

"Join the Navy, See the World?"

"The Army. But it was something like that. Trained in New Jersey, saw that neck of the woods. Had me some adventures in the Apple."

"So you liked it?"

"Yeah. Like I said, saw a thing or two. Any more, I stick pretty close to home. Go to Eugene sometimes to give Tyrone a hand. That's about it."

Vernon took a gulp of beer, watched his kids, and James and Junior, playing to one side. Then he said quite deliberately: "So what brings you here?" She wondered if this was what he'd been leading up to.

"It just kind of happened," she said. "One thing led to another."

"You were gonna have an experience."

Libby agreed, then wished she hadn't. She took another sip, feeling wary, hurt.

Diane, over by the trunk of the red car, said "Vern, would you give me a hand?" Vernon got up to help Diane unload the trunk. They set the food out on the table—potato salad and apple salad, chicken and more beer, and a big chocolate cake with chocolate frosting and shreds of coconut and "Happy Birthday, Tyrone" written across the top. Junior tugged at his father's arm, pointed. Tyrone saw the cake, his name on it, all the others looking at him, and started to beam. Phyllis set to peeling the Saran Wrap off the food containers and laying everything out. Diane poked through a cardboard box.

"Shit!" she said. "I forgot the knife. My beautiful cake!"

"Take it easy." said Vernon. "We'll make do."

"Ain't nothin' to fuss over. I could always go back for one,"

53

Phyllis volunteered. How Phyllis loved to drive that car, thought Libby.

"That's silly," Vernon said. "Relax." He opened another beer, thrust it at Diane. "Compliments of Little River Inn," he said.

"Oh Lord!" said Diane, throwing back her head and her free hand in a sudden laugh. Phyllis and Vernon, Ross and the man in the orange shirt started giggling too. Tyrone looked like he didn't exactly get it, but was happy anyway, and laughed. Diane gave Ross a shove in the arm, ribbing him, it seemed.

"Crazy fool," Libby made out, and "Phinney" (Phyllis was laughing so hard now she gasped for air) and "cracker" and more "Lord!"'s among all the rest of the words she didn't catch and couldn't understand—because of their accents, because they were talking fast and over each other and laughing on top of it, because she hadn't been there. Must be some white guy at the local tavern they were making fun of, something that happened one night at Little River Inn. They laughed at Phinney, at crackers, at whites, at Libby, she thought. At their next picnic, she'd be the joke. Or maybe was even now; maybe stuck in among all those things she couldn't understand were code words about her, the Goldilocks, the sightseer, the white girl Tyrone had dragged along. What a damn giggle: that Tyrone hadn't bothered to explain to her how far it was, when he asked her to come, and that Phyllis either thought she knew or—just to be ornery— didn't tell.

Their laughter, interruptions, shouts tumbled all over each other behind Libby as she stepped away from the trees into the open and the strongest sun. The smell of barbecuing meat wafted on the air. She looked across the park, searching for a still spot, wanting it all to stop, and walked down the slope to the water fountain by the men with the lawn chairs. She turned the silver handle at the side of it, stuck her mouth down into the arc of water. It was clean and cold on her throat, probably straight off a snow melt. Someone came up behind Libby, fumbled for the handle too.

"Thirsty," he said. Libby turned. Tyrone grinned. He'd run across the clearing after her. "Sorry, Libby," he said earnestly. "We goin' soon."

"Thanks for telling me. Thanks a million."

"Sorry. Come on. Have cake."

Libby looked up the slope. They were all in the same loose clump, carrying on, full of their small town in-jokes and their jive talk; the kids were in a furious little pine cone fight nearby.

"Alright, alright," she said. "I'll come. You go on back." She turned away and bent for another drink. She could hear the group of men, and "Rocky Raccoon" from their truck radio.

"Radial?"

"Brand new radials, suspension, shocks!"

There was something familiar about them, and she realized she understood each word, even though she knew nothing about cars. She let go of the handle, rotated part way, looked at the men, and when she stepped away from the fountain, she faced them. Tyrone reached after her, his hand on her shoulder. Libby shrugged him off, hard.

"Don't, Tyrone." She could see the men's faces. They had all stopped talking and were watching her push Tyrone away. One guy stood with his boot slung up on the edge of the grate in a husky pose. They looked predatory and alert. She felt small and dirty in their eyes—for coming so near, for being with this black guy, for not being a man. None of them said a thing; they waited. She had to say something.

"Would you happen to have a spare knife?" Oh God, did that sound stupid! Like borrowing a cup of sugar.

They were looking both at her and beyond her at Tyrone, who'd hung back.

"That group there is having a birthday party," she hurried to explain. "But they need a knife for the cake. Do you have a spare one?"

The man standing up looked at Libby—a real slow look—and reached for an aluminum knife on the picnic table, held it out to her. When she put out her hand he held the knife back, ever so slightly, so she had to pull.

"Keep it," he said. "Maybe you'll need it."

Laughter. Some of them took sucks of beer. One guy kicked a burning log with his boot and sparks flew up. As she turned to go they started talking again among themselves behind her, the sound of their words like dirtballs hitting her from behind as she recrossed the clearing—slowly at first as Tyrone followed beside her pulling at her arm, then at a lope toward the top. It was OK now. She'd handled it right and Diane could even cut her cake with a real knife. Libby grinned as she held it upright in front of her to show Diane, because Phyllis and Vernon, Ross and Diane and the rest had all stopped what they were doing and were looking, each one of them, straight at Libby. Also at Tyrone. Also, across the clearing, at the men. When she delivered the knife to Diane it was quiet.

"Christ!" someone hissed—the man who'd come with Ross.

"Whose idea was she anyway?" Diane asked.

Phyllis, beside her, said "Make a wild guess," then turned to her brother sarcastically: "Happy Birthday, Tyrone. You done got us in a mess again."

"That bunch looks hungry," Diane said. "You can tell it, Vernon." She went over to the side where the kids were and gathered them back near the tables.

Vernon stayed seated on the bench, as if by will power. "What's the big idea?" he asked Libby. "What's the big fucking idea?"

Libby looked at this man, the one who'd tried to be nice. He was scowling, scolding her, and she didn't know why, what she'd done that was that awful, why they hated her so much. "The cake..." she started to explain.

"Fuck the cake," Phyllis growled, from beside Vernon, almost right on top of Libby, gesturing in Libby's direction and off in the air in wild, excited gestures. "What you figure these crackers do, they see him bothering you? Any of them, any one in this place, just say a nigger's up here bothering a white girl, state police be up here on our ass in one minute, someone be hauled away."

"At least!" someone else agreed.

"You born yesterday?" Phyllis demanded. "Can't you see those mens? You got no business!"

Phyllis paused, fixing Libby with a venomous look. The other woman stared too, and the men, even the kids stared, with their mouths open; Tyrone stared. Libby's face was flushed with blood. Her heart was thumping under her breast. She had never thought of it just that way: any one of the white people in the park who got it into their head could make the call. They did do things like that; it had happened; it could happen now. Just one call, and anyone could do it; she could. Or those men could come over and really start something. And it would be her fault, for being so dumb. Her breath was caught, trapped between her mouth and her lungs. Her ears and face burned. She started shaking, trying to keep from crying.

Vernon, Ross, the man who worked with Ross all took another good look across the clearing. The men were still staring back, and talking among themselves, and gesturing. But they hadn't moved from their places around the fire. Vernon turned, took the knife from Diane, started carving the birthday cake in big angry chunks. "C'mon y'all. Go on with our party."

"I don't feel right," Diane said. "The kids."

"C'mon, Diane," Vernon said to her sternly "We got a right. We'll keep an eye out." He put chunks of cake on napkins, placed them in the kids' hands. They all said "Happy Birthday" to Tyrone and they had the cake, their little party. But the spirit of the thing had changed. When Diane and Vernon started packing up, Tyrone herded the boys into the Pontiac, and Phyllis and the Speeds and Libby left the park.

Libby sat with James against one shoulder, her head tilted back on the seat. She bent her forearms over her face and focused her eyes between her arms at the dark brown vinyl that was above her head and all around. Underneath, the tires made a steady sound on the pavement, in counterpoint to Phyllis and Tyrone's voices that rose to peaks and subsided in an unpredictable rhythm.

"Please," Libby thought, "just leave us be; let us get home," when they stopped for a fillup at a roadside service station, and a grisled white man came to Phyllis' window, went around to pump the gas, and came back for the money. She wished she were invisible.

They pulled back onto the highway and Libby shut her eyes against Phyllis and Tyrone's argument, her exhaustion, the excitement and strangeness that had still not gone away, the constant moving whir inside and all around her. Sun streamed in the windows and Libby watched the bright red—probably her own blood—it created behind her eyelids. In the changing pulse of bright, then dark, she saw an image of herself as a woman of glass on a rafting trip wishing the boulders and white water all around their rubber boat would disappear and stop still so she wouldn't shatter. When Junior and James exchanged shoves or body blows on the seat beside her, the reverberations passed through Libby. The Pontiac hurtled down its chute between the evergreens, toward Eugene.

Beach Party

We climb the bleached stairs to the boardwalk and, as the sea comes into full view, I picture the perfect end to our weekend reunion: sand trickles from my sister's and brother's shoes once they're back in Denver and New York; they're reminded of the beach where our earliest summers passed like sand through a fist; they're reminded of me.

All morning in the car we told family stories by theme: accidents we had as kids; the love-hate relationship between our parents; then defecation-urination-sex-and-sexuality—a long series of body stories. My husband Lewis, at the wheel, is the model listener, goading us with questions. We recount to him our bouts with pinworms, the exploits of the Barbie and Ken dolls, who seemed to me to be forever occupied, along with my brother and sister, in the baby blue bedroom they shared at home when they were little.

"We're having a beach party," Teddy yelled through the locked door the day I first demanded what they were doing in there. The morning seemed to wear on and so did their party; the sun climbed the sky and when it grew too hot they came out—Nadine and Teddy still giggling, Barbie and Ken still naked, Barbie's once smooth and nipple-less breasts permanently mutilated by a set of teeth marks.

"Ken did it," Teddy said, as he laid Barbie, Nadine laid Ken, out for the night as if for a wake in the hinged wood box father had constructed. Whenever I asked them about the beach parties I always felt they were withholding information from me, even when they told me Barbie had let Ken play with her instrument panel, that she had touched his pubicoos, that he'd felt her bucket butt. These were code words from a private language used by Teddy and Nadine, and by me, the eldest, the one who'd had my parents completely to myself for four years before he came along, then she, in dizzyingly rapid succession.

Theodore was small at birth. He was ugly, remained purplish awhile, and made mountains of dirty diapers my mother washed by hand in an enamel tub.

"That's what babies do, Florence. Thank God you're past that," she said, her voice heavy with relief and possibly with warning as she taught me to fold the clean diapers into the shape of triangles without tops. One day as mother was changing him on the bathroom counter he peed into the air. It arched wildly and landed in a puddle clear across the room. Mother handed me a rag and asked me to wipe it. She claims to have caught me hovering over him later that day, intent on mutilating him.

"Flo, you're scrambling things," Nadine corrects. In her windbreaker and sunglasses she's the first one on the boardwalk and she's staring across the railing at the sea. "I don't believe you had castration fantasies *that* early. Even that ditty about Mussolini we didn't learn till later—from that little dink across the street," she adds. She recites in a tuneless voice, as illustration, the song we chanted with the neighborhood kids out on the dirt street the city sprayed with oil every summer to keep the dust down: "Whistle while you work/Krushchev is a jerk/Mussolini bit his weenie/Now it doesn't work."

"It's OK, Nade," Ted says good naturedly from Nadine's other side, soothing away her trace of distemper. "Let Flo tell the story."

And since it's he who's in danger in this episode, or because he's always had so much pull with Nadine, she assents, by way of her famous silence.

I stop a moment, nursing my delicate feelings, noticing the gulls caw abrasively as if for our attention, beyond the tan sand, at the edge of the changing tide. We watch them plunge into the churning blue-green water, quarreling or standing self-satisfied and full of fish on the black rock breakwater that juts out into the sea. It is only May and the beach is still virtually empty of sun bathers, swimmers. I remember the blanket I've packed away in the trunk, in case we want to lie around, but Lewis ponts at the wind, tells me to leave it be. I'm terribly glad he came along—to silently take my part, I imagine, and to give us the opportunity to recount everything out loud. It is just like my husband to carve himself a niche.

Even-voiced over the gulls and crashing surf I go on about blankets and discovery, ostensibly addressing Lewis: "Daddy used to mow the lawn with a power mower he revved up with a cord. He had a canvas drop cloth he dumped the clippings on as the basket behind the blades filled up. One day Teddy and Nadine were inspecting each other under the cloth. I caught them with their pants down."

"And what did you do?" Lewis prompts, tipping his head in a gesture of interest, though I could swear I've told him this story before.

"She blackmailed us," Nadine says.

"Not blackmailed, exactly."

"You're hedging, Florence," says Ted, cracking a proud smile. My sister and I make the obligatory groan in unison at his pun on hedges and lawns. Other people, hearing his far-fetched jokes, just chalk him up as odd. To set the matter straight, I never blackmailed them, only requested a few errands. Right about then I needed some extra leverage. I'd seen the first signs of rebellion when Teddy prevented me from eating the cookies he'd brought from the kitchen to the television room. Next thing I knew they would be refusing to fetch things when I said.

And the truth was I was around ten by then and accumulating sins of my own. When Teddy lay on the couch in front of the tv and little Shirley Temple danced the times tables down the spiralling lighthouse stairs, corkscrew curls flying, *I* was bouncing on Teddy. Stretched out on top of him, I took care our bodies rubbed and rubbed. But I wasn't doing anything, not really, not anything specific he could pin on me. Over the back of the couch I kept an eye out for Daddy come to tell us we'd watched enough "boob tube" for the day, for our mother when she brought the tv trays and dinner. The room was full of Shirley's high-pitched voice and Captain January's old one. My head was swirling.

"She'd jump me so fast I never knew what hit me," Ted swears, surveying the view—the waves or a heeling sloop, I can't tell which—in a grand abstract manner I recognize in him. It is

Ted's way of reasserting his sexual disinterest. Nadine and I thought he was gay long before she asked him. She's the direct one, sometimes bordering on indiscreet, the one who left the little note in the pages of my diary, near the spine, at the place where I'd written about kissing my first boyfriend in the park, his brushing against my nipples.

"Tssk, tssk, Natasha," it said. I was Natasha. Teddy was Boris. She was our baby Bornatash. Other times I was Zelda Norwich and I gave advice.

"Remember this, Teddy? 'Dear Zelda Norwich: I have a problem. My girdle's killing me. Come up and see me about it sometime.'" How exquisite were Teddy's imitations of Mae West—camp and he didn't know it. Before that, at around three, it had been pop beads, tutus and high heels, his life as a lady.

"I *was* good, wasn't I?" Ted says, putting a hand to the side of his head of dark thick hair, as if straightening his blond curls, about to be Mae again. I take a look at Ted, his oxford shirt typically buttoned nearly to the neck, as there's something unusual in his self-expressive outburst. He must be feeling released by the sea air or our visit to be carrying on so, but I'm not sure I like it and I hear myself saying: "Oh please, Theodore. Don't corrupt Lewis. He's pleased as punch thinking he tried everything at least once in his wild youth."

Lewis chortles, gratefully I think. And Ted—I can actually feel him retreat back into a faraway, private look of his. Nadine, next to Ted, turns her face downwards in a narrowed, concentrated expression typical of her—at her canvas deck shoes, the boardwalk slats, the clean cold sand down below. Both have strong cheekbones, long unhandsome noses, square chins. I frame their profiles in relation to each other and snap the picture in my mind for the day one of them passes on, should I outlive them. Which of us will go first, I bother to wonder, and how?

Nadine is the first to descend to the beach. The sand has crept up, covering the bottom step. It grabs hold of, sucks, at her thick pale ankles. She fights it, trudging with heavy steps toward the edge of the water, wheeling her arms through the crisp air in what seems to me to be a strained imitation of delight. It seems as if Nadine has always been fighting something, and that with time it's solidified into her way of being in the world. Ted moves

62

toward me once she's down the steps, resting his hand on my shoulder. He watches her solid, wide-hipped, swaying body and I imagine him thinking: "what a shame that Clifford left her with those kids." But Ted never actually thinks of Nadine as I do or as I expect him to.

Now, as if to rescue her, as if staying with me is too odd, Teddy breaks away from my side and follows Nadine, catches up with her. Their two backs sway from side to side, near each other, as they struggle through the loose sand. I imagine, in his hands, a pail and shovel. I remember the summer they were nine and ten and went away each morning to a day camp.

"You're lucky. You get to sleep late," mother consoled me in a brittle, chirpy voice. But one morning I saw them out the window waiting for the bus that picked them up. I got the impression they were arguing: Nadine was shaking her balled fists at Teddy. Yet even then they sat so close to each other on the curb that I pictured them Siamese, joined at the hip, with two heads but only one heart between them.

I lean on Lewis. A gust of wind sneaks up on us, slaps us in the face, ruffling Lewis' already-receding hairline, and I feel preparation in my husband's body, then Lewis raising a hand and yelling "Hello, boy!" to the collie who's galloping in ecstasy along the sand. "Glorious, isn't it, Flo?" he asks, referring to everything, in the full, easy way he has. I look at him, seeing myself as so much more cautious than he. I wonder if I was ever as aimless and open.

Once, while doing target practice outside town, father put a gun in my hand. I was eleven, wearing a red coat that fit too snugly, and trembled at the dense feel of the gun.

"Give it a try, Flo," he said. "You're big enough to handle it." Teddy and Nadine watched without speaking. "Go on," he said, and pointed at the big black bird that hung in the sky above us. I aimed and when I pulled the trigger the bird tumbled out of the air, lay stony on the dirt.

There's a picture, taken later that afternoon, that Ted found yesterday, leafing through the old album. In it Nade and Teddy appear buoyant, like little redeemed children of God, standing against the car. My own face, lips, compress to a single line pulling down to one side; my shoulders look pinched by the coat.

"Look at us, the three little brats," Ted remarked, then came back to the cribbage game we were playing in teams.

"Twenty-four," Nadine counted, laying down a card.

So casual, the both of them, as if they weren't perfectly aware that the back of the photo had at some point been labelled "The day Flo killed a bird," as if our faces in the picture didn't contain that fact. Ted threw down his card, pegged two for thirty-one. My heart wasn't in it any more. Nadine had been wrong to pick me for a partner.

Now, high above the beach, a large white cloud moves swiftly out to sea; gulls, abandoning the sand, travel in its shadow. I follow their line of flight toward the boundaries between sand and water, then water and sky.

"Come on back!" I yell, but not loud enough against the wind, waving my brother and sister in. Way out on the end of the breakwater they are one dark shape against the blue and I have the idea they're old lovers, planning a party, and have eyes only for each other.

The Tree Farm

All the way from Philadelphia to the tree farm mother and daughter fought. All the way Quinn sat surprised and watchful in the front passenger seat, feeling as though she herself might be drained when it was over.

It was Sheila who had decided they should leave the city by early afternoon. She pulled up at 30th Street Station right at 12, as planned, motioned Quinn with a beckoning flick of a finger into the car.

"Hi stranger," she said, giving a warm bear hug across Quinn's bag, on the seat between them, then held out her cheek till Quinn pecked it. "Now to get the girls." Sheila knew the streets so well they reached the school in no time.

Two teenagers were standing on the curb in front of the building as they pulled up. One wore a large woven bag slung from one shoulder of her Levi jacket, a scowl on her face. Quinn recognized Sunsh—short for Sunshine—immediately, recalling the once small-for-her-age seven-year-old who'd raced around the tree farm in Oshkosh overalls. The other girl was tall and pretty, with a straight brown braid hanging down between her shoulder blades. Sheila waved. They climbed in. Sunsh slammed the door hard behind her.

"Hello kid," Quinn ventured affectionately, as Sheila opened her door, dragged the bag off the seat, and stowed it in the trunk. Quinn regretted immediately the word 'kid.' Sunsh must be 14 by now, a real teenager, and the bang had been to announce her bad mood.

"Hi," Sunsh answered, barely audible, as her mother got back in the car.

"Ain't talkin' while the flavor lasts!" Sheila chimed in promptly, trying to be jovial. "You'll thank me, Sunsh," Sheila continued, apparently taking up some quarrel where they'd left off. "We'll miss the worst of the traffic."

Sunsh seemed unappeased. And no sooner had they reached the freeway than a guy in a Corvette passed on the right at break-neck speed and cut sharply into their lane, oblivious to a motor-cycle cruising along right in front of them. When he saw the bike he braked suddenly, and hard. The Toyota nearly climbed his back.

"Mom!" Sunsh said—alarmed, accusing, infecting the car with tension.

"I see him!" Sheila snapped back, rattled. "When you get your license I'll let you drive, OK? Right now it's my turn." But the close call had scared Quinn too. She felt angry and instinc-tively, irrationally blamed Sunsh. "I bet there was some cute guy in class who Sunsh didn't want to leave. Am I right, Linda?" Sheila probed, peering back through the mirror. Linda loyally re-frained from answering. "And by the way, Sunsh, what ever happened to that lovely boy Timothy?"

"Last week a girl accidentally broke 'that lovely boy's' pot," Sunsh sneered, "and he threatened to 'slap her tits together.' "

"Good God, you're kidding!. . . . Anyway," Sheila persisted, after a small pause to recover, "I bet you've got your eye on *some-one* there."

"Oh Mom!" Sunsh protested. "We were firing today!"

"Sunshine, I didn't *make* you miss pottery. Didn't I say you girls could take a bus out tonight if you wanted? Or you could have stayed home, for that matter. It was *your choice!*"

Sheila the anarchist trying to incorporate the principles of indi-vidual responsibility into her childrearing—how typical, and un-changed. At this thought Quinn felt both comfort and alarm. The same quartz crystal still hung from the same black cord around Sheila's neck. She still drove barefoot, sneakers cast off between the two front seats, as she had in the old days. And now she'd worked it out to go back to the tree farm as summer caretaker, while the owners were away. This trip was to bring up the first carload of stuff. In a few weeks they'd bring everything else, and stay on.

"Some choice!" Sunsh said. "You know I hate buses. *Hate,*" she repeated for emphasis. "They make me nauseous. . . . And it's called 'ceramics,' not 'pottery.' " The complaint about getting nauseous bothered Quinn. She thought of teenagers as fickle and self-involved; they faintly repelled her. "You could have waited two hours. What's the big rush? What's it to you?"

Quinn considered that the rush might have been about herself. She remembered Sheila's prediction that they'd have a wonderful Memorial Day weekend together. "For auld lang syne," she had enticed Quinn over the phone.

It had been Memorial Day, 1973, that Quinn had gone to visit Allison, a friend from high school, and the other women on the tree farm. The first evening of the visit, after saying they needed more womanpower on the place, and again the next day, showing Quinn the stand of evergreens being grown for Christmas trees, Sheila had said: "So you're staying." Half option, half instruction: it had been compelling. Ever since, when people asked her about that time in her life, Quinn told them she had moved to the tree farm within a week because she knew suddenly she needed to live lightly on the earth with women. But it seemed to her now that what had cinched it was a tone of voice.

A vast petrochemical plant loomed up outside the car window at the side of the highway. Its tanks were huge and rounded like puffballs; its silver and white pipes cut complex shapes against the sky. At one time Quinn could have mired herself in depression almost at will by looking at this landscape of pollution-making monuments. She wondered if she were growing or just morally eroding. At one time, too, she told herself, she'd lived on women's land, considered herself part of the cutting edge. Now she felt like a tame, harmless adventurer-gone-home. Quinn felt so normal that it frightened her.

The chemical plant disappeared behind them and Quinn heard Sheila saying that getting stuck in traffic gave her headaches. "Like two bull goats," she told Sunsh, with a wry smile Quinn caught from the side. Sheila took her hands from the wheel to butt the knuckles together in the center of her forehead, like the headache sufferer in the old tv commercial. "Would you have wanted that?"

And Sunsh plunged on, in dead earnest: "You always tell me

that I give you a headache. So what's the difference?''

"You've got a point there," Sheila laughed generously. Sheila could give, let go, slip out of anger into laughter and back again with ease. It was something Quinn had always admired about her. One of the *many* things, Quinn amended, flinching at the thought. For a year and a half, or a year (it was hard to define the end; it had faded away slowly, painfully, not ended with a bang) they had been lovers. Even now Quinn could recall the pride she'd felt about her special relationship to Sheila, along with specific moments of humiliation she had endured because of it. Even now she could still recall the sting of a particularly direct, fierce, and exasperated demand Sheila made one morning six years ago: with a hand on one hip so that her blue bathrobe hung unevenly below her knees, Sheila had said:

"You're not the first one ever to put me on a pedestal, Quinn. But I liked you. I figured you'd grow out of it." Quinn felt devastated; Sheila had looked solitary and almost desperate as she paused, then asked, as if betrayed: "How was I to know you wouldn't?"

The intonation matched disturbingly the one in Sheila's voice now as she asked Sunsh with annoyance: "Can't you be a little more grown up about it?"

"Why should I?" Sunsh said angrily. "Besides, I didn't want to stay home!"

It would be comforting to side unequivocally with one of them, Quinn thought. No doubt Linda was sure of where she stood, sided squarely with Sunsh.

"You're mother's a trip," Linda might tell her pal, once they were alone. And maybe Sunsh, to counter any trace of admiration in Linda's comment, would point out how much of a pain her mother was, how dumb and predictable her lesbian feminist enthusiasms.

"Capital L, capital F." she'd stress.

A slim windy road through the woods brought them the final stretch to the tree farm. Quinn recognized its turns, the side roads joining the main one, the pond that bred bullfrogs and mosquitoes.

"There's Edna Frazer's," Sheila said, for Quinn's benefit, as their former neighbor's prim frame house came into view. Sheila seemed to think that five years away, a new life in New York City, must have eroded all Quinn's memories of the tree farm, though she herself had been away for four. It seemed she had never really understood how Quinn thought, what things faded first for her, what stuck. The road plunged down under the canopy of leaves that shaded it for the last hundred yards before the house.

One time, on their way home from a weekend outing, Quinn's parents had stopped to visit her at the tree farm. Her father had waited at the top of this road; her mother had come down on foot and appeared in the clearing without warning.

"I left your father in the car," she'd said pointedly, as if hoping for an invitation for him, as she climbed to the porch of the main house in her sturdy deck shoes, her crisp checkered shorts. "He wasn't sure he'd be welcome."

An awkward moment followed. People looked in Sheila's direction to see if she'd volunteer an invitation to him. She didn't; no one did.

Someone, probably Redwing, instead invited Quinn's mother with strained hospitality to stay to dinner. She agreed to "just a bite" and helped set the table on the screened-in porch. They started the meal with their customary moment of silence—heads bowed and hands joined in a circle. Quinn was seated between her mother and Sheila. Sheila's hands were hard from hoeing and weeding and pushing wheelbarrows. Her mother's were small and smooth, the way Quinn remembered them from childhood—making tight worried gestures, or idle on her apron, or pressed together in church like an obedient child's: "Our Father, who art in heaven, hallowed be thy name . . ."

The silent prayer on the porch ended; they let go of each other's hands. It stayed horribly quiet for one prolonged moment except for the sound of mosquitoes through the screen, of women mumbling requests for tamari or couscous.

Afterwards, Quinn walked her mother up the hill to the car, said hello to her father. Her mother got in, then leaned out the window and pointed at Quinn's feet, dropping her voice suddenly to a low, private whisper as if there were someone else there besides family.

"Please don't throw those out ever," she requested. "I want to have them. As a memento. Of this terrible period."

Quinn looked down at her dusty toes, the sandals with the tire tread soles that Sheila had made and had said she could keep.

"So long, Quinn," her mother said then, as if, having found a symbol to contain her pain, she could now bear to leave. Quinn watched, astonished and crestfallen, as the family Dodge lumbered away.

She still kept those sandals, buried in a corner of her apartment.

The Toyota shuddered, then gasped to a complete halt as Sheila pulled the car up in front of the house, turned off the ignition, pronounced happily: "Free at last!" The back doors popped open instantaneously; the girls jumped out like prisoners released.

Let me get the gas on," Sheila said as she slipped out of the driver's seat and bounded toward the house, her red-brown trousers, lavender bandana, and tiny pouch on a long string leaving the impression of color and discord in her wake. Linda and Sunsh grabbed their bags and followed, disappeared up the stairway just inside the door. As she unpacked the car, Quinn could hear one of the girls opening an upstairs window, Sunsh giggling inside.

Quinn searched the car's interior—among driftwood pieces, gay community leaflets, seaweed candies wrapped in edible rice papers, and "This Insults Women" stickers—for anything she'd missed. An orange day-glow frisbee protruded from under the seat. She tugged at it and the frisbee came free; a prehistoric-looking jawbreaker rolled out from somewhere underneath the seat. Quinn picked the jawbreaker off the mat and flung it full force into the bushes, laughing. What would Sheila be like at 80? she wondered. And was struck, as she carried in an armload, by the knowledge that what she wanted this weekend was Sheila to herself.

Once the "girloids," as Sheila called them, had gotten settled in the bedroom upstairs they came down to say they were going for a walk.

"While there's still light," said Sunsh.

"Be back before dark then," Sheila instructed.

Sunsh threw back a scowl as she shut the screen door, as if to say: "Yeah, yeah, we're not kids anymore, or idiots!"

Quinn admired Sheila for not saying the obvious to Sunsh, but noticed Sheila's need to say it out loud once the girls had disappeared up the drive: "They'd be twiddling their thumbs in the dark instead if we'd waited all day to leave Philly." Quinn giggled, but she found herself giggling alone, for Sheila abruptly turned reflective, almost sad: "Look what a nasty old crab I've become." She cast a glance at Quinn, looking self-conscious. Suddenly she bounded toward the door, threw it open and yelled up the drive, where the girls had been: "Watch out, girl, or I'll slap your tits together!"

Sheila collapsed against the doorway, laughing tensely, as Quinn stood staring at her. In this same house, on this tree farm, in the old days, they had spoken, behaved, differently, almost decorously. And because of Sheila. It had always seemed that Sheila approved of, even expected, the right-minded tone that had been achieved and sustained on the tree farm. Intrigued and confused now, Quinn searched Sheila's face for whatever it was that seemed aggressive, even hostile, in this outburst of irreverence. But Sheila would not stand still for this examination; she was on a roll.

"C'mon," she said, "this old crab needs daylight too," and grabbed Quinn by the elbow and swept her along. "Let's take a look."

They walked through an open yard next to the house, where their big garden had once been. Now the space was occupied by a car body and a woodpile covered by a tarp. The path starting on the far side of the yard cut through some tall grass and past the apple tree that would drop bushels of fruit all over the ground later in the summer.

In hot weather, as Sunsh picked its apples intently off the ground, Tamara used to sneak up and empty a pail of water over Sunsh's unsuspecting head and flat, bare chest. From the cabin Quinn and Sheila would hear Sunsh's shrill cries of protest and delight. They knew this was one of Tamara's little ways of showing how close she was with Sunsh, how irrelevant Sheila and Quinn were to anyone's contentment. The other women objected

71

more directly to Sheila's absence from the main house, though they did concede it was small for six.

Twenty yards past the cabin, Sheila and Quinn now came to the stand of commercially-cultivated evergreens. All the trees were straight and well-formed; they grew in regular rows to an even height and stood apart from the wild profusion of honeysuckle and hardwoods that covered the nearby ground and the surrounding countryside. Quinn played the game of narrowing her eyes till the edge between the cultivated rows and the woods blurred, and it became one continuous, unbroken landscape. When she opened her eyes, it changed back. She noticed nearby, off to themselves, two trees perhaps three feet high, different from the others.

"What are these?" she asked, fingering their stiff, narrow, pointy-tipped leaves.

"Yew. Sunsh planted those before we left here. Someone in town told her the wood is especially nice for carving. Maybe she can use them now after all." Quinn imagined the elegant wood spoons, boxes, chess figures Sunsh would make in Industrial Arts class. "Can you imagine planting something so slow-growing as a tree—at that age? Remember how you were at eight?" Sheila asked, with what sounded like motherly pride.

And Quinn remembered something she'd once known about Sunsh—how uniquely determined, almost relentless she could be. Once someone had shown her how to curl dandelion stems in water and Sunsh went out and picked virtually every dandelion within a quarter mile radius. Later she'd appeared for lunch, head covered by a pile of wet, pale green curls like an eccentric belle.

"Those classes of hers must really be important to her," Quinn said to Sheila in a commiserating tone of voice.

"It's not just that," Sheila answered, and Quinn felt herself deflating in a way she remembered from the old days, whenever Sheila had spoken to her gruffly. "It's a lot of things she's mad at me about." Sunsh resented the years in a commune instead of a nuclear family, growing up without her father. Sheila had left that difficult marriage when Sunsh was still a baby, and soon afterwards became, as she put it, "an Amazon—one of the Amazon nation."

"Have you and Sunsh talked about it?" Quinn asked, carefully putting more question than suggestion into her tone.

"No, we haven't talked. But we should. We're going to," Sheila said unequivocally. And Quinn, to her own surprise, felt left out instead of pleased that Sheila had come around. They used to quarrel over Quinn's desire to discuss things, Sheila's insistence that talking didn't help. Plus here at last was Sheila sounding committed to someone, the way she'd never been with Quinn. On the way back to the clearing, Quinn asked where the owners had gone for the summer, what their plans were for the farm; but Sheila didn't answer, perhaps hadn't even heard the question. Inside the house Sheila moved about furrowing her brow and talking out loud—not to Quinn, but to herself—about a pie she wanted to make for the girls, even though Quinn remembered Sheila as a rather lackadaisical cook.

Miffed, and hungry for nature, Quinn went outside. In the dirt beside the porch she saw a bent up trowel; she pulled it out and began digging around the flowers. It was relaxing to yank out crabby little weeds with stubborn roots and shake them free of dirt.

After a few minutes Sheila came trotting out with a multicolored string hammock, probably Mexican, from one of her trips to the women's land in the southwest where Allison now lived. She found the two hooks—one screwed into the house and one tied to a nearby tree—and hung the thing.

"You want the hammock?" Sheila asked, suddenly attentive, as if to make up for her earlier lapse of attention. There was a look in Sheila's eyes—needy and vulnerable, almost. "You can rock and dream about that new girlfriend of yours," she joked.

"I'm content," Quinn said firmly as she faced Sheila, a clump of weeds dangling from one hand. "Don't you want it?"

"I've got to go into town. I promised Sunsh they could have chicken pot pies for dinner, and I forgot to buy them. She loves those things," Sheila said, and curled her lip with resignation, as if she had hoped Sunsh would opt for wheat berries and steamed vegetables. "Actually," Sheila said, drawing the word out as she glanced at Quinn, "would you come with me?"

There was the thought of cashiers and concrete and sidewalks, when she'd longed for a retreat from all that. There was being in the car again. There was the thought that the hammock had been a pretext to ask this favor. And there was the hopeful look in Sheila's face, that Quinn wanted to deny; she had hardly ever denied Sheila. Quinn was aware of a wincing pleasure as she shook her head, "no," saw Sheila's hopefulness collapse.

Even as Quinn finished speaking she heard Sheila add hurriedly: "It's alright, though, if you prefer to stay," then watched her retreat around the corner of the house, strands of long dark brown hair flying away from her head. Sheila had her motherly responsibilities to fulfill, Quinn thought, disquieted. She heard the car engine turn over, the gravel pop under the tires as the Toyota pulled out.

The wicked pleasure that she had been feeling slipped away from her; the trowel felt heavy and ridiculous in her hand and the scraggly flower bed seemed a sad substitute for their glorious old garden. Quinn left the trowel on the ground, stood and looked hard at the yard. The woodpile was bathed in late afternoon light. So was the path. She found herself retracing her steps through the grass and out past the apple tree. She paused in front of the cabin, then mounted its two plank steps, lifted the latch.

The door opened and Quinn stopped still. In place of the original, small panes in the wall opposite there was a large plate glass window. It filled the room with light and a view of the strange, silent rows of evergreens outside. The fist that formed in her chest took her by surprise. She had imagined only the comforting sight of familiar objects: the butcher block, wood stove, chair, rug, mattress.

Quinn saw herself again on the mattress by the window, holding onto Sheila. Sheila's fingers ran along Quinn's breasts, and side, and thigh, then slipped inside her, pushed deep, as Quinn rode them. A breeze, and the sound of crickets, came in the open window from the woods. She used to make sounds but had always been too shy and tongue-tied to form words; if Sheila said something, even something as simple as Quinn's name spoken tenderly, Quinn would shudder.

Sheila had always slept soundly after they made love, and Quinn had almost always been restless and unable to sleep. She would get up, watch Sheila, so thin between the sheets; her fingers seemed tiny, clutching the cloth. Sheila must not be woken, Quinn would think protectively. And would tiptoe across the carpet, lift Sheila's robe gingerly from the hook on the back of the door. It was the first thing Sheila put on in the morning, the last she took off at night. When she wore it open, without a sash, you could see Sheila's breasts, one heavier than the other. Or else she'd gather the blue-green cloth in her fingers to hold it closed. Its color was dazzling, almost iridescent, its cut simple and elegant. One day in a burst of enthusiasm (she was the collective's oldest and most impassioned member, and its leader, though they never spoke of leaders) Sheila had stencilled interlocking women's symbols on its back with lavender fabric paint.

"My dyke robe," Sheila called it; Quinn had thought of it as Sheila's fish robe, too. At the hem, below the dyke symbols, was a border design of fish with wide-eyed expressions of permanent surprise, circling her loyally in a single direction. Quinn thought of the fish as intelligent creatures; she assigned them emotions. She imagined their pleasure as Sheila put the robe on and as she wore it; then, when she took it off for the night and hung it on the hook, their sense of abandonment.

Quinn had known the exact number of steps it took to cross the carpet to the door, the number down from the porch to the ground. Clutching the front of the robe, she became a smaller, younger replica of Sheila. She knew the direction the outhouse door swung, took care to gather the robe up to keep its hem from catching on splinters or falling down the hole as she squatted.

Returning from the outhouse, Quinn used to shut the cabin door quietly behind her, hang up the robe and scoot quickly across the room and under the covers. Once, instead, she stood awhile near the mattress and watched Sheila turn in her sleep. She saw she might have to fight to reclaim her side of the bed; she took off the robe, laid it over Sheila, climbed back in.

The sun had dropped just behind the tops of the trees as Quinn returned to the house, hearing the sounds of voices that floated out from the windows. Maybe they were arguing again. Then she heard laughter, and Sunsh's distinct above the others'. She pulled open the screen door and followed the sounds to the kitchen. Linda was seated at the kitchen table arranging a set of toothpicks in a row. A pot of water was beginning to heat over the stove's blue flame. Sunsh and Sheila were stabbing with forks at a single pot pie that rested on the edge of the stove, like two giant children squabbling over a dessert.

"Quinn, she's stealing my Swanson's" Sheila protested theatrically, giggling, then said: "Go ahead and hog it all. We've got better things to eat."

"Where were you when we got home, anyway?" Sunsh demanded.

"Town. You know who I saw? Gretchen. She said the Fairfield kid will be here all summer."

"Ick," Sunsh said quickly. "I bet he's a hulk by now." She explained to Linda: "They're the ones who live down the next drive. He's a creepola."

"More than a creepola," Sheila said. "Gretchen calls him 'a handsome charmer with a streak of evil.' She says to avoid him if we can. He better not come onto this property," she said threateningly. Sheila actually looked worried. "Anyway, what about you girloids?"

"What?"

"Where'd *you* go?"

"To the pond awhile," Linda said. "But mostly on the bridge."

"The overpass," Sunsh said. "We were waving at cars."

"Yeah, a lot of them waved back and honked," Linda explained enthusiastically.

"That's nice. So you had a good time."

"Yeah," Linda agreed.

Sheila asked them, in a vaguely strained, scout leaderish tone untypical of her: "If you could have a banner and hang it from the overpass, what would you say on it?"

Sunsh and Linda looked blankly at each other.

"Hi!" Sunsh exclaimed.

"Love ya!" said Linda.

"Oh, you must really be in a good mood toward the world!" Sheila told them, clucking. Linda took the kettle off the flame, poured the water into two mugs with Snoopy pictured on their sides, dunked the tea bag first in one, then the other, wound the string around the spoon and wet bag, and squeezed.

"What about 'No Nukes: Weapons, Power, or Families'?"

Sheila asked with enthusiasm.

"That's you!" Sunsh retorted venomously, and like that said it all. She made a let's-get-out-of-here gesture to Linda and left the room, holding her steaming mug in front of her as Linda followed two steps behind. Sheila looked dejected; she called out after them into the hallway: "Sunsh, you want to visit Edna Frazer this weekend?"

"She's a drag," Sunsh answered back.

Sheila started to say something, then stopped herself. "Well, *we're* going," she said instead, meaning herself and Quinn.

"Anyone who's female, even if she's a real bore, she thinks is God!" they heard Sunsh tell Linda at the bottom of the stairway. And Quinn, aware of Sunsh's conspiratorial tone, thought that if Sheila for any reason decided they should leave Philly before Sunsh finished high school, Sunsh would never forgive her. Quinn wondered whether Sunsh, like her mother, might thrive on social contact yet always come out hungry. She pictured Sunsh clinging, fiercely as a little animal in a tree, to her world of school hallways, hamburger joints, and friends.

From out of her pouch Sheila produced a picture postcard of a woman on a flying horse, a fluted clam shell, a small silver labyris, and a vial of volcanic ash that might have been mistaken at first glance for cocaine.

"Fire, air, earth, water," she said, crouching, as she arranged the objects thoughtfully on a straw mat on the floor. Quinn took the book of matches with the cover reading "Dykes Ignite," that Sheila held out to her, and lit two small candles, one on either side of their altar. The candles' glow enlarged the intimate circle of light cast by the fire, in front of which they'd stretched their sleeping bags.

It would be fun, Sheila had decided, to stay in the cabin one more time. "It's like clubhouses when you were a kid," Sheila said, charming in her playfulness. "Feels cozy, doesn't it, Quinn?" Quinn thought of Sunsh, in the upper room of the main house, and wondered if Sunsh resented her.

Sheila intended to use the cabin as a work space through the summer, to design and silkscreen feminist and anti-nuclear posters—when not looking after Sunsh and Linda. The girls were going to look for jobs in the area, but they'd probably get part-time ones; they'd be around a lot with time on their hands.

Sheila rooted through her knapsack, pulled out a book, then her familiar blue robe looking only slightly more frayed than before, then an unopened pack of Juicy Fruit, then the thing she was hunting for: a cassette tape of Edna Frazer talking about the area, her long life, what she thought of "all you girls" living down at the tree farm. The tape never failed to bring back memories of their days at the farm. Quinn had heard it last in March, the weekend Sheila visited New York. They did a lot of other things too: went to some photo galleries and to an off-Broadway matinee and to a reading at a women's bookstore. A few women at the reading had come up to greet Quinn; one had asked after Camilla.

Quinn remembered an odd moment of silence on the subway home that seemed about more than just the noisiness of the ride. It was the two of them digesting something new: Sheila had always been not only older than Quinn by nine years, but a mother, a militant and a star. Now Sheila needed Quinn to guide her around New York. Now Sheila was on the sidelines and Quinn had someone new—her first real love since she'd left the tree farm.

There was some relative of envy afoot now, too, as Sheila, cross-legged on her sleeping bag, said: "So you think you've met Miss Right."

"Yes," Quinn agreed, wondering if her lingering feelings for Sheila amounted to a betrayal of Camilla. And then she added: "I guess you could call her that."

"A married woman and you're not going to hold me?" Sheila asked—coy, teasing, and quoting words ("aren't you going to hold me?" that Quinn had used once when Sheila started seeing someone else besides her.

"I'll hold you," Quinn said, a little defensively, then added, to lighten things: "But I won't hem your slips." Sheila smiled thin-ly. "What about you? What's going on? I guess there's the friction with Sunsh?"

"There's that. Or maybe it's that kid next door." Sheila had had hopes of running around the tree farm again this summer topless, like an Amazon. "It's going to be a hard summer in some

78

ways,'' Sheila said, and looked off.

Quinn reached out instinctively to put her arms around Sheila, and pulled near. Sheila's body felt tense and almost unnaturally still, as if it held back a great flood of tears. Quinn longed for their release as if they were her own.

Over Sheila's shoulder, out the window, the dark sky and darker evergreens laid jigsaw shapes against each other. Before long the moon would rise, just there, and Sheila's body would relax. She would fall asleep, and Quinn would arrange the robe once more over Sheila's shoulders, wondering what person she herself might become if—when—what had charged this devotional act was gone.

In Praise of Creeping Things

When my mother's knitting needles made their angry clicks,
when the reading light above my father, stiff in his chair, trained a
yellow beam onto his page, I stood at my parents' second story
window and watched the tent caterpillars spinning their white
net. High in the branches of the trees that formed a screen against
the neighbors, the nest was visible to me from the window, but
difficult to spot from the ground below.

So when my father walked the lawn, setting up sprinklers to
move and stop like clockwork, he never saw the nest until I told
him where to look. It was then that he went after the caterpillars.
It was then that I monitored his handiwork from above: the clip-
pers opening at the end of the pole, severing the web; the white
tent falling to the ground; the waiting can of gasoline he dunked it
in; the gold flames jumping as he set the nest on fire.

After the caterpillars were wiped out, my father went hunting.
For deer? For fowl? Don't be a ninny. Father hunted the back
yard for moles. He examined their dirt mounds, figured possible
maps of their tunnels below; he took his time. He bought mole
bombs at a gardening store. He set the sticks in the mouths of the
tunnels. He lit the fuses. The rest was up to your imagination: the
frantic mole fleeing as the fumes surged toward it, then lying
down defeated in its tomb.

Mother preferred elbow grease and offensive measures to
bombs and gas after the fact. She scanned the territory out by the
walk and mailbox and under the branches of the tall birches that
the landscaper had ordered. She wore high rubber boots and a
heavy sweater. She watched the hairline of the grass where the
moles' humped grey backs first broke through the crust, before

81

they'd made their damnable heaps in the front yard, facing the street. She walked pitchfork in hand, observant. It revolted her but it had to be done, she said, glancing toward the street, her voice thin and unconvinced. Still, she stabbed deep into their bodies, she stopped them cold.

And I was the distressed creature watching, running to the front yard, the back, comparing the successes and satisfactions of their methods, judging mother and father by their separate, self-chosen means.

Which was better? I can't answer that. Don't ask me to measure muscle against ingenuity, like dogs against cats. I can say something, though, about this: why mother would have preferred her means, father his; why mother would prefer the work of heart, adrenalin, lungs and arms, and the undeniable guilt as she stabbed clear through to the fuzzy creature's heart—she whose life seemed always separate, vague and lost. While father, after so many daily bothers at the company, could figure, set the bombs, and have it be far away down deep where the mole actually passed out in its blanket of gas and died.

My parents—no green thumbs, I might mention—were trying to keep the yard nice. They were giving a lot of parties that were important to my father's career and the subject of much tension and loud arguments. The house had to be clean; the place settings, the menu, and the yard had to be just right. Molehills were undesirable, and the leavings of stray dogs. This was before the leash laws, at a time when dogs still ran loose through the neighborhood at night leaving piles on lawns, baying, rooting in garbage cans, eating food off porch steps as the guests inside the houses simmered down into after-dinner drinks and dirty jokes not intended for the ears of children.

I can see my mother, lingering in the living room among the laughers, or coming into the kitchen where I eavesdropped, her arms weighed down with serving dishes like she was a heavy-laden coat stand. She meant to set them down somewhere among the vast clutter that already filled the counters, as it did at every party, and only at parties. I picture her confused eyes and small scowl as she moved unfamiliarly in the usually immaculate room, searching for a place to put the meat platter, the vegetable dish, and the rest of her delicately balanced objects.

"Come help me," I remember her saying once, overwhelmed. "Don't just stand there. Sometimes I really can't stand you—or him!—or anyone. You're all beasts." I helped her, and as soon as all the dishes were on the counter she said, "Finish making that milkshake and run along." They hadn't meant to have me. But once I'd come nonetheless they made the best of me; I had my assets.

One of my assets was that I could climb like a tiny monkey. I hoisted myself up onto the counter to reach the shelf with the chocolate sauce while mother fussed below with the dripping serving spoons. From up there I was high enough to look out the window. I saw Bender, the fat, aged bulldog owned by the Chamblisses next door as he gobbled the first of three perfect golden-crusted dessert pies mother had set out there to cool.

I couldn't quite make out in the near darkness, but could imagine, his jowls red with the luscious raspberry meat and seeds. It came as a surprise to me, who had never known a dog and had no idea they could go for fruits and sweets.

I have to own, though, that yes, I certainly did see the bulldog's deed, and in time to have saved the day had I alarmed mother. But something about it caught me unawares and fascinated me. I mean the lights at the end of the walk shined cheerily; the dinner guests' cars were parked at the curb like docile, obedient cows; and the guests themselves were snickering, father among them, in the front room vacuumed and dusted and straightened up for the occasion—while Bender gobbled at the delicacies.

What did mother do when she went to the porch for the pies that would crown a perfect meal? Naturally she looked stunned and called father in. She told him in a loud whisper. She showed him the sweet red mess on the top cement step. Then I watched her go back into that party room. And I saw, from my low vantage point near the doorway, the little place where her smile curdled at the corner as she apologized in a way that made all the guests laugh.

I swear, though, I don't remember which came first—hating Bender or him ruining the pies, if it was before or after that that we came to curse the ways of "man's best friend." I don't remember when it was we started the mortal crusade against the Chambliss dog, hating the very thought of his mouth, shiny black and dripping. The human creature is easily molded by what's around her, and as a child, I must admit, I did my best to make "Bender" a household word of hate. I got mileage out of reporting his every trespass against the premises—not immediately, always, but eventually. Even when I needn't have, when I half hated myself for doing it, so that I felt the need to make it up to Bender, later, when we finally got acquainted.

It was I, for instance, who knew and told why the decorative evergreens died. They were low-growing pines, their roots bound in gunnysacks, that father brought home from the nursery and set down like punctuation marks at the corners of the house. Yet it's dogs, they say, who "mark" their territory. So why not come right out with it? All right, father was marking the corners of his house with shrubs, like little low parapets.

This I knew, somehow, and so appreciated Bender's brashness those autumn mornings when I saw him move along through the fog that encased and hid him, like a huge, corpulent caterpillar inside its web. He moved through the yard, careful and curious, sniffing at the edge where the grass stopped and the curved planting areas strewn with cedar bark began, at the empty air above the window well, at the smell of pebbles and tiny green weeds that grew down there.

I followed inside the house, moving from window to window to keep him in view. I watched him as he reached the azalea bushes and snarfled at their bright fallen flowers that had slid away from the pistils like a glove from a hand. Then he sniffed at the low lamps that lighted the walk, and at the three mushrooms I knew had come up through the cedar chips intended to discourage weeds, and then at the startling bursts of upright pine needles like those painted on Japanese screens.

And in spite of all the nasty things I'd ever said or heard against Bender's rolls of fat, I saw him lift his leg delicately to piss on the pine. Not only one day but twice or seven times, twenty or twenty-seven, till the thing turned piss yellow and withered up and died. I tattled, and my parents began using slingshots and BBs on Bender and the others when the neighbors weren't around.

The Chamblisses, especially, were in their front yard a lot. Mrs. knitted baby clothes in a lawn chair while Mr. worked the flower beds. They were childless people. She had been pregnant with a baby at least three times that I'd heard of, and once she got pretty far along, but every one of her babies came out dead.

"But then they finally succeeded," father cracked one day. "She had a deformed one with extra legs." He was talking about old Bender, someone else's reject that they had brought home one day from the pound. The Chamblisses were indulgent parents. For his frequent walks, they dressed Bender in a wool coat Mrs. had knitted, and they let him bay in the back yard all night long. "Like the Hound of the Baskervilles," father said, imitating Bender.

My parents liked this joke about the neighbors' mongrel offspring. When the Chamblisses passed, with Bender on a leash, mom would say, "would you look at that! I think Bender's going to have a sibling!" Then they'd peer through the window trying to decide if Mrs. Chambliss was pregnant with a second four-legged child or if they were being misled by her coat.

Mrs. Chambliss never ended up with a human child. I always imagined that made her sad, so I was surprised at how cheerful she seemed the first time I really looked at her, the day she approached me at the mailboxes. She wanted to know, would I be interested in taking care of their dog Bender while they went away on a trip? They would pay me, she promised, and the idea of earning my own money for once convinced me, even though I had always known Bender as that fat slug of a dog next door with slime dripping from every end, and even though mother and father would hate for me to get involved. They cracked a few jokes, but they let me.

It wasn't hard, either. The Chamblisses had Bender on a long chain attached to his doghouse. All I had to do was squeeze through the hedge where the stems stood wide apart, fill his bowl with chunks of hard brown food they had set in a dry place under the eaves, make sure he had fresh water, and move his piles off the lawn.

The first night I did it right after my own dinner. I remember it like yesterday because of how my father teased when I came home. He said he'd watched me across the hedge lifting Bender's piles so tenderly, like fragile fresh-baked pastries, off the Chamblisses' lawn between a pair of sticks. He'd seen old Bender come oozing up to me on the end of his chain, he told mother, laughing, and startle me so that I stuck my arm out straight and awkward to touch his neck and his rolls of fat. Dropping the pile, he told mother, right on my foot. Mother laughed a shrill, scaredish kind of laugh as I looked down, shame-faced, blushing, at the faint stain still left on my tennis shoe.

After that I only went over when the sky had turned blue-black and the first stars were stuck up there as sweet in the firmament as Bender the bulldog seemed, for all his slime and bad habits, lying there by his shed. I talked to him while I poured his food, the chunks clinking against the side of the bowl in the dark. And I talked while the food disappeared with sharp pulverizing sounds in his jaw. Then he rubbed up against me with his pushed-in face like a shovel had whacked him. And I confessed all the terrible names I'd called him, and my part in causing the slingshot assaults launched against him, now, whenever they saw him approach our yard.

It was mysterious, I could almost say sublime, how he seemed to forgive me. He didn't snarl or snap, nor once crow with vengeance, so to speak, as I picked up his piles with sticks to remove them. Instead he cuddled up with his appreciative wet nose and well-meaning, down-turned, drooling mouth. Which was more, I felt, than my mother would do if I messed up her kitchen; it was more than father had done when I threw off the timing on his sprinklers. And those sins of mine seemed like tiny specks compared to the malice I had harbored against the dog.

I'd go home to bed and think about it. Hunched up under the covers, I alternately embraced and fought off a new feeling about Bender that I felt sure would cause me troubles the next time they brought out the slingshot or cursed his name. Sometimes I listened to the house creak, or watched light move across my curtains from some auction or sale being advertised with big search-beams that swept across the sky like the wail of Bender that rose up for the vacationing, absent Chamblisses, or for me, maybe, maybe for me.

In the mornings father and mother, looking tired, would say it was getting worse. They didn't say what "it" was, but I knew. It was Bender. They said his baying caused them hard times "making nookie," and insomnia. Father said the racket was enough to make his hair fall out.

"They ought to put him out of his misery," father said. Mother said, beside herself: "I could strangle him." They fantasized plots against his life—standard stuff, stuff I didn't listen to but went to school and did my chores: dusted furniture, salted slugs, watched for stray dogs, fed Bender and talked to him.

The last night before the Chamblisses came home there was a light wind, no moon, and Bender began to bay. This time he really did bay deep into the night—at the no-moon, the wind, for me, for the Chamblisses, for the souls of bombed moles and the ruined splendors of tent caterpillar civilizations. For whoever and whatever a dog finds to bay about. A few hours before dawn he finally cut it out, probably tired out and deep asleep, because there wasn't another bay or bark out of him in the remaining hours of darkness or the next day, or that night, when I saw the Chamblisses' car coming back into their drive.

Awhile later they went out to feed Bender and greet him. Then the baying started up. It was the Chamblisses, though, not Bender, wailing away across the hedge. It was Mr. Chambliss with his flashlight, and the two of them dragging Bender's fat white body, like a belly-up dead slug, into the back porch light. Old Bender had died away the last night he was under my care. I was afraid they might think it was my fault—but Bender was so old, they told me, choked up, they hadn't thought he was long for this world, anyway. So I guess for them, after the first shock of it, maybe it wasn't so horrible.

But I took it hard. I didn't have a pet turtle or jumping bean, even, to make up for this hound I had watched and fed and talked to. And I wanted to find out just how Bender had died. I figured if it was by suffocating or poisoning that would tell me a thing or two. I sucked in my breath and curled into a ball like a potato bug and prayed for all the creeping things.

And from then on I have never betrayed them nor presumed to end their misery so long as it was no worse than my own. And I began to sing their praises.